TROPIC OF CLEO

TROPIC
OF CLEO

RICK HOLMES

CUTTING EDGE

ISBN-13: 978-1-962896-25-2

Published by
Cutting Edge Books
PO Box 8212
Calabasas, CA 91372
www.cuttingedgebooks.com

CHAPTER ONE

THE ISLAND LAY BENEATH the right wing of the airliner like the back of a gnarled, aged hand in the sea. Thin lines of surf stretched along the beaches, and as the plane banked, letting down for the airport, a white sail came into view below, driving for the harbor.

"Fasten your seat belt, Cleo," Harry Gregory said.

Her husband's voice pulled her out of her reverie, and Cleo turned from the window to see that the warning sign had flashed on at the forward end of the passenger compartment. She stubbed out her cigarette and drew the belt over her lap.

"Come on, baby," Harry said, smiling. "What the hell are you pouting about? Look down there. *Look* at it! Paradise. A real tropical paradise!"

"Then why are all the natives going to New York as fast as they can get out?"

His grin broadened. "Still sore, aren't you?"

Cleo looked away, out the window of the plane, and jerked her belt tight. "Sore?" she said, whirling around to face him, her green eyes smoldering. "You're damned right I'm sore! I don't like being dragged off to some Godforsaken island in the middle of nowhere, for no reason at all! I want to be back where things are happening, where there are people."

"Any particular people, Cleo?"

Her expression changed into one of suspicion. "Say it, Harry. You've had something on your mind for quite a while now."

Their eyes held for several seconds. Then the smile came back to his face and he looked past her. "We're letting down. We're almost there."

Cleo was about to pursue it further but she knew Harry Gregory. When he changed the subject, nothing—not reason, baiting or cajoling—could get him to talk about something he did not wish to discuss.

She turned back to the window. The plane was dropping low, the wing seeming to shift back and forth as the pilot adjusted his course to line up with the runway. The end of the field flashed past beneath and then the plane was at the end of the runway and there was the slight jerk as the wheels touched down. To Cleo it was like the short stroke of a knife blade, severing her from the places she wanted to be and things she wanted to do.

Tropics. It brought to her mind Gaugin, or Somerset Maugham, or films of camouflaged soldiers someplace in a jungle. The thing was completely revolting to her. She hadn't even particularly liked Florida, though there was life and action there.

The big plane turned off the runway and rolled swiftly along the taxi strip toward the terminal. The airport looked like all others to Cleo—little tractors moving about, gasoline trucks pulling up to the wings of planes, refueling.

She unfastened her seat belt and took a cigarette from her purse.

"The no-smoking sign is still on, Cleo," Harry said.

"To hell with the no-smoking sign." She clicked her lighter and the young stewardess leaned across Harry, smiling politely. "Sorry, Mrs. Gregory. You can light up in a few seconds."

"I'll light up now—"

Harry lifted his right hand and took the cigarette from her mouth, crumpling it and letting it drop to the floor. "My wife is sorry. She didn't realize the sign was still on."

The uniformed girl let her eyes linger understandingly on Harry for a moment, and then she nodded and moved away down the aisle.

"The little bitch," Cleo muttered. "Seventy or eighty people on the plane and she spots the one with money like a bird dog spots a covey of quail."

The plane came to a halt and passengers began moving down the aisle toward the door. The door to the forward compartment opened and a blond young man in a uniform came out, followed by an older man who was adjusting an airline officer's cap.

The younger man's gaze touched on Cleo and stopped. His look would have been unusually flattering to any woman who was not accustomed to receiving such scrutiny. He smiled at Cleo, his eyes flicking momentarily to Harry and back to Cleo, as if asking if she was with the man. She started to smile back, decided that would be encouragement, and there was no time for that now. The young flier was obviously not interested in a brother-sister relationship, not the way his eyes went to her breasts. His elbow nudged his companion. Cleo looked away and stepped out into the aisle.

After a short wait inside the terminal building the luggage was claimed and they went out to the cab stand.

Harry relinquished the two bags to a driver. "Caribee Hotel," he said.

"*Si,*" the cab driver said.

They rode away from the airport in silence. After a while Cleo said, "Now will you tell me what this trip is all about, Harry?"

"Just think of it as a vacation, Cleo. Just the two of us, getting away from everything for a while."

"I know better than that," she said. "You've been acting like a spy with a guilty conscience. Is this place our destination?"

"I've bought a boat. We're taking a cruise—south through the islands."

She turned and looked at him in astonishment. "You've done *what?*"

"Bought a boat. A nice little forty-two footer, twin engines, the works. We're going down to St. Ursula where I've rented a

3

house. They say the cruising down there in the islands is absolutely wonderful—hundreds of little islands to explore."

Cleo dropped her cigarette on the floor and crushed it out beneath her shoe. "You must be out of your mind, Harry."

He grinned. "You'll see. We're picking the boat up first thing tomorrow morning, and off we go."

"Just us? You and I?"

He nodded, still grinning. "Romantic, isn't it?"

"Are you serious, Harry? A—a *boat?*"

"Why not? I did a lot of boating before we were married, and I was in the navy, an officer." Harry reached over and put his hand on hers. "And don't worry about getting lonely. We're having guests."

"I'm sure of it—you *have* taken leave of your senses. And just how long is this little island idyll supposed to go on?"

"It depends. I don't want you to concern your pretty little self with things like that. Leave all the details to me. You just relax and enjoy yourself."

She stared at him, making an intense effort to refrain from exploding in anger. Finally she said, "I ought to take the next plane back to the States."

"You do that, Cleo darling, and that will be the end of it. You've gotten used to money, and my personal opinion is that you couldn't get along without it. And with your dubious talents as an actress all you'd do would be to end up sleeping around for bit parts in television—"

"I ought to—"

"Oh, shut up, Cleo. You're not going to do a damn thing, we both know that."

The cab turned off the street. "Caribee Hotel, señor," the driver said. The cab pulled up in front of the hotel, a massive modernistic structure of aluminum and glass.

They went inside to the desk. "Gregory," Harry said to the clerk. "We have a suite reserved."

The clerk consulted his bookings. "Harry J. Gregory?"

"That's right."

The clerk smiled broadly. "Ah, yes, Mr. Gregory! Your suite is ready. Suite Seven-ten ocean front."

"Have them send up something to drink, Harry," Cleo said.

"We'd like a couple of martinis sent up right away," Harry told the clerk.

The man nodded ingratiatingly as a bellhop appeared and took the key.

"Make that a pitcher of martinis," Cleo said to the clerk. "And get it up here right away."

"Certainly, Mrs. Gregory! Right away!"

The elevator ride was swift and silent. The suite was directly across the hall from the elevator. The boy opened the door and ushered them in. He put the bags down and opened the sliding glass doors leading out onto a balcony. "Is a very nice view from here," he said.

Cleo went out on the balcony. A warm breeze blew in from the vast expanse of the ocean spread before her as far as the horizon.

"That is the fortress there, señora," said the boy, pointing off to the left.

Cleo looked in the direction he indicated and saw the massive gray ruins on the promontory overlooking the harbor mouth. Beyond, on the sea outside the harbor, a sailboat ran free before the wind, coming into port. Cleo wondered idly if it was the one she had seen from the plane.

There was a knock at the door and the bellboy hurried back inside to answer it. It was a second bellhop, with a tray and the drinks Cleo had ordered. He came in and put them on a table.

"Señor Gregory," he said, reaching into his jacket pocket, "a cablegram for you, sir. The desk clerk he forgot it." The boy handed Harry a yellow envelope. Gregory took it quickly, tipped the boy and tore the envelope open.

Cleo helped herself to a large martini and drank it avidly, as though taking some potion for relief of pain.

When the two bellhops were gone, she looked at Harry. "What's the cablegram all about?"

Still preoccupied with the message, he looked up. "What? What did you say?"

"The wire," she said. "Was it something that might take us out of this tropical paradise and back to civilization?"

"Merely business," Harry said, stuffing the paper into his pocket. "Nothing that would be of the slightest interest to you."

"Oh." She lifted her glass, drained it, refilled it from the pitcher and went out onto the balcony again.

"What do you say we go down to the pool for a swim before dinner?" Harry suggested.

Cleo sipped her drink and looked down from the balcony. The hotel pool was directly below. Beyond it were cabanas, and then the beach and the sea. Quite a number of people were lounging about the pool. A dark-haired girl in a yellow bikini went off the diving board and entered the water cleanly, with barely a splash.

"I don't think I'd care to, Harry."

She turned and came back inside the suite. The gin and vermouth were softening her. She felt a great deal better than she had when they got there. In fact, she was very nearly amenable to staying, getting this crazy trip over with on Harry's terms, and then getting back home.

"Is your bathing suit in your bag?" she said. "I think it was in the things that you shipped ahead."

"I bought another one in Miami, remember?"

No, she didn't remember, but that was of no importance. Miami was a little vague all around. There had been a big fight in Miami, and she had gotten quite drunk.

Cleo walked across the living room and stopped at the bedroom door. Harry had the suitcase open and was digging through the clothes. He lifted out a pair of sky-blue trunks.

Cleo took a long swallow of her drink. "Sure you don't want to stay up here and have another drink?" she asked. "It's very relaxing. Very."

"I know. But I feel like a swim. And after that I feel like a big steak."

"And I feel like a neglected wife," Cleo said, emptying the glass again and looking about for the pitcher.

Harry unbuttoned his shirt and took it off. Then he unzipped his pants, pulled them off and draped them over the foot of the bed. Cleo looked at him standing there in his shorts. She tilted her head this way and that.

"You know, Harry, you're a remarkably well preserved man for your age."

He shot her a glance. "For my age? Barely forty-three, darling. Barely forty-three. The prime of life."

She walked to him, smiling, and put her glass down on the night table beside the bed. She pushed her hands over his shoulders and clasped them loosely behind his head.

"Actions, Harry, speak louder than words."

He smiled back at her, reaching out and pulling her against him. Cleo made a little sound in her throat and pulled his face down to hers. "Don't go down to the pool. Let's stay up here. We can call down and have some more drinks sent up." She unclasped her hands from behind his neck and moved them down to the elastic band of his shorts, smiling as she became aware that her actions were rousing him.

"It unbuttons in the back," she whispered, and felt his hands begin to unfasten the buttons of her dress. She closed her eyes, the alcohol bringing a vague, comfortable dizziness to her brain. The dress loosened across her back and, with a little wiggling motion, she let it fall to the floor at her feet. The nylon slip followed it and then her brassiere and panties.

"Just like it used to be, Harry," she murmured, stirring strongly against him, feeling the hollowness pulling inside her, the need, the urgent need that always seemed to be a part of her no matter what the time of day, no matter where she might be, whether in the quiet intimacy of a hotel room, or crossing a busy street in traffic. It was always there, more demanding than hunger or thirst, always crying out.

His hands moved on her body, slowly, almost disinterestedly. Cleo moved her own hands up his back, pulling him to her, trying to make his response more than a mechanical thing, something more human than a chemical reaction.

"It used to be good with us, Harry ... so good ... didn't it?"

When had the deterioration begun? What had happened? She tried to shake the thoughts from her mind. Yet, deep in the vagueness of her thinking she seemed to know that this in itself was part of the fault, this not wanting to think of causes and reasons. Her defense had always been offense, and so had Harry's. With both of them continually on the offensive, what possible chance was there for a solution to anything?

Her hands trembled against Harry's broad back, moving in little circles on his smooth skin. Start fresh. Make a new beginning. Give in a little. How do you admit you're wrong?

"Harry ... " Her words caught inside her, swept away in the surging flood of passion. His hard body pressed against her, enfolding her whole being, swallowing her up. Her thoughts made way for pure feeling, her mind became simply a focal point for sensation as Harry eased her down to the bed.

The coverlet was rough against her naked skin and, fleetingly, she thought the sheet would be better, but the thought vanished as his hands moved gently over her body, cupping her breast, making every nerve end come startlingly alive.

She smiled at him and then, incongruously, she giggled.

Harry paused. "What's funny?"

She pulled him back to her and placed his hand on her breast again. "I was thinking, who needs a swimming pool?"

He laughed and Cleo pulled his face to hers, her lips parted, her tongue darting. She pulled her mouth away, her breath quickening.

"Harry! Now, Harry—*now!*"

His body moved above her in response. He was good when he wanted to be. She dug her heels into the rough-textured coverlet, her head thrown back tightly against the pillow, and pulled him to her. This was her blessing and her curse—the two were inseparable. Seeking release and yet not wanting it. Knowing and remembering nothing but this vacuum within her demanding to be filled.

Yes! Yes! Yes!

She heard her voice repeating the word over and over, faster and faster. A symphony without music, beginning slowly, easily, tenderly, and building gradually, always building, but with deliberation, so as to prolong that promise which lay ahead.

Her nails dug at him, pulling him to her, into her. *"Harry..."* Her body arched tautly, closer, closer.

He stopped, his body rigid, cold and controlled, and then he raised up away from her and looked down into her passion-clouded eyes.

"Was it this way with Crawford in his apartment, Cleo? Did you call out to me, or was it 'Johnny'?"

Crawford? she thought confusedly. Her mind was not ready for thought. *How could he know about Johnny Crawford? He was out of town on business when that happened, so how could he know?*

But that was not important, how he knew, or even whether he knew. What was important was *naw*, the present, this moment when she was hanging somewhere a million miles in space, drifting in expectation. Cleo lifted her body upward and tried to bring him back to her.

"Please, Harry. I can't stand that—you know I can't stand that. *Please!*"

She began to move, beginning slowly again, trying to find a beginning, though she knew it was useless, This was his rack, his thumbscrew, Harry's punishment.

Without hesitation, he pulled free of her and got up from the bed. He picked up his bathing trunks. "There's the phone right there by the bed. Call him, Cleo. He's three thousand miles away, but call him. Tell him I've gone down for a swim and the coast is clear." Smiling, he let his eyes move over her naked body. "Tell him the pump is thoroughly primed."

"You filthy, sadistic bastard!" she screamed, quickly turning away and burying her face in the pillow, not wanting to give him the additional satisfaction of seeing her complete frustration. She lay there gripping the pillow until she heard the door close as he left the suite.

Slowly, she turned over and opened her eyes. She lay there for several minutes, staring up at the ceiling. How many ceilings had she looked up at, in how many frames of mind? Nine years.

Her mind reached back for her first meeting with Harry Gregory. Cleo was nineteen, but far from being a wide-eyed kid. She was in summer stock, and the company was playing Atlanta. She was introduced to Harry at a party one night. Maybe that had been the start of the trouble, the first misstep, because she got the word that he had money, and when he showed a strong interest in her, Cleo made up her mind that her chance had come.

For a month, Harry used every tactic short of rape to get her into bed, but she was as nonyielding as a vestal virgin. Something had to give, she knew that. Harry, at 34, was well along the way to becoming a confirmed bachelor. His father had died recently and Harry had taken over the presidency of the chain of dry-goods stores left him by his father.

But bachelors were not asexual. Cleo's experience had taught her that lesson. When confronted with a girl who would not give in they had three choices: they could walk away, they could become friends, or they could become exbachelors.

Six weeks after that first meeting, Harry asked her to marry him and Cleo accepted. The merry-go-round started without delay. They honeymooned in Europe for four months, a fabulous time, but even then she seemed to sense the antagonism in Harry.

Outwardly, everything was fine. They behaved as a pair of wealthy newlyweds would be expected to behave, which was precisely as poor newlyweds would behave, only between more expensive sheets. There was nothing tangible about the feeling Cleo came to know in those weeks, but without question it was there. It was as if Harry had had to buy a ticket when all along he'd expected a free pass.

At first it was little more than a vague and occasional petulance, and in it Cleo took a certain amount of perverse pleasure, knowing that she had been the winner. But time went by and the game became more intense, with Harry seeking out advantages and, upon finding them, utilizing them to the fullest.

He never became so obvious or crass as to resort to cutting off charge accounts or expenses of any kind. He preferred subtlety, and from the beginning he found his greatest weapon of reprisal to be, ironically, the very thing he had married Cleo for. Cleo, to her husband's delight, in more than one way, was a sexpot.

Cleo stirred on the bed. She drew in a deep, tremulous breath and sat up. The pain she felt, she had known before. It was this that had driven her in desperation to such men as Johnny Crawford, this and the feeling that in infidelity she was also striking back at Harry. The pain was more than physical. It pervaded her whole being, lingered far down inside her like some malignant fire. She was incomplete, unfulfilled—an uncrossed *t*, a dotless *i*.

At times such as this, she asked herself why she stayed with Harry. The obvious answer was that Harry had money. Another answer was, habit. Unless a situation was completely intolerable, the *staus quo* was generally more acceptable than change. It had even occurred to Cleo that she had developed a strain of masochism to complement Harry's sadism.

Wearily, feeling as though she had been run part way through a wringer and then backed out, she got up from the bed and leaned to pick up her scattered clothes from the floor. *The bastard,* she thought. *The unmitigated bastard. He knows what he can do to me. Oh, the lousy—*

Across the room she glimpsed her reflection in the mirror of the partially open bathroom door. She straightened and, with idle curiosity, stood erect and regarded the image of herself. Her body was good. No, it was better than that. It was excellent. It must take great will for Harry to deny her. She lifted her hands from her sides and touched the rose-tipped breasts that stood large and firm. There would come a day when gravity would prevail, but so far it had been balked.

She let her hands slide down to her waist, tiny by comparison, across her belly and down her thighs. Her hands moved restlessly against her legs for a moment, and suddenly she clenched them into fists and jerked them away. Turning quickly, she went into the other room where she had left the martini pitcher. Not bothering to find a glass, she lifted the pitcher in both hands and drank deeply and with purpose.

CHAPTER TWO

HARRY WAS ALREADY DRESSED when he shook her awake the following morning.

"Come on, Cleo. Wake up. We've got to get a move on. I've already called the boatyard and everything's ready."

With considerable effort, she got out of bed and went to the dresser. There was one cigarette left. She lit it and crumpled the empty pack. The smoke was harsh and unsatisfying. Her head ached dully and there was a decided queasiness to her stomach.

"I'll meet you in the dining room," Harry said. "Have your bag ready for the boy when he comes up."

Cleo nodded and ground out the cigarette in the ash tray. "Order me a Bloody Mary, will you?"

Harry went out, closing the door. Cleo dressed slowly, and when she was done, she approached the mirror and looked closely at her face. She had been drinking too much, that was obvious. It was beginning to show, particularly around the eyes. She shook her head and moved back; a crumpled yellow paper lying behind the wastebasket caught her eye. She picked it up and spread it flat on the dresser top. It was the cablegram Harry had received. She looked at it with mounting curiosity. It had been sent from Hamburg:

> HEINRICH AND I ARRIVE ST. URSULA
> 15TH VIA MAIL BOAT. HAVE EVERYTHING
> READY. TIME MAY BE FACTOR.
>
> FREEMAN

She reread it, puzzled, and then she recalled Harry's having said something about guests. But the cablegram did not sound like the acknowledgment of a guest. She knew no one by the name of either Heinrich or Freeman.

After a moment, she shrugged and dropped the paper into the wastebasket. She took one more glance in the mirror and went downstairs to the dining room.

Her drink was on the table and she finished it quickly. Harry was drinking a cup of coffee, apparently already having finished eating.

"You took long enough," he remarked.

Cleo put the glass down on the table. "I don't want any breakfast. I'm ready to go whenever you are."

"Good. I've already checked us out."

Their bags had, been brought down to the lobby, and they went out and engaged the first cab in the line.

"Hermanos Salazar Marina," Harry said to the cabbie. "You know where that is?"

"*Si, señor.* The other side of the harbor."

"Then let's get going," Harry said, settling back in the seat beside Cleo. He turned toward his wife as the cab lurched out into the street. "Hung?"

Cleo rubbed her forehead. "The Bloody Mary helped some, but not enough."

"You shouldn't have loaded up last night," Harry said. "At least you should have eaten dinner. You knew we were starting early this morning."

She turned and looked at him. "There wasn't anything else to do last night so I got drunk."

He grinned. "You're hot about what happened."

"If I'm hot, it's about what didn't happen."

"Just a little object lesson, sweet. That's all it was."

"I wish I had the guts to walk out on you, you sonofabitch."

"No need to act like a frustrated child, Cleo. Besides, who knows but what I'll save you the decision and throw you out one of these days."

"It'll never happen, but I almost wish it would."

"You're mighty sure of yourself."

"It's just that I know you, Harry. You'd never throw away anything you thought someone else wanted. And you'd rather exact punishment than take revenge." She turned and stared out the window of the cab. "Like yesterday."

"That really bugged you, didn't it? You're oversexed, Cleo. I think you've got a touch of nymphomania. Is sex really so important to you?"

"Is it so *un*important to you?" she countered hotly. "It's not my invention, Harry! It was here when I came!" This was leading nowhere. It was completely pointless. She sighed and rubbed her forehead. "This hangover's killing me. I'd like a drink."

Harry leaned forward and tapped the driver on the shoulder. "Stop at the next liquor store."

The driver nodded and, after two more blocks, pulled to the curb. Harry handed him a ten-dollar bill. "Get a fifth of rum, light rum, and get a couple of cokes."

Cleo closed her eyes and waited. The driver came back and passed the bottles through the window to Harry. He opened the fifth and handed it to Cleo. She didn't like drinking from a bottle, but this was no time for propriety and she tipped it up to her mouth and took a long swallow, chasing it quickly with the soft drink. The rum burned her throat and, for a moment, she did not think she would be able to keep it down. But the feeling of nausea passed and she relaxed and slumped back against the seat.

"We can proceed now?" the driver inquired.

Harry nodded. They went on in silence, the cab roaring through the streets, heedless of other vehicles which ventured into its path. After a while Cleo took another drink from the bottle.

"Better go easy on that stuff," Harry said. "We've got a long boat ride ahead of us, and seasickness is no more enjoyable than a hangover."

"I'll try to remember that," she said, taking another pull at the bottle.

Some time later the cab turned off the street and entered the grounds of the boatyard. They pulled to a stop before a paint-peeled white building. A faded sign above the door read, *Hermanos Salazar Marina.*

"Harry—" Cleo said suddenly as they were getting out of the cab. "Harry, let me go back! Please let me go back!"

He looked at her with mild amusement. "Back to the States? Just because you've got yourself a hangover? That's a laugh. You'd be in somebody's bed before you were five minutes off the plane!"

"I *swear,* Harry! I'll live like a nun, only let me go back! Please!"

"You go on in the office there and wait. I see one of the Salazar brothers out on the dock."

"Harry—"

"That's enough whimpering, Cleo. Do as I say. That boat's pulling out of here in a few minutes and we're going to be on it. Both of us."

Cleo took the bottle of rum and went into the building. The room was dirty, cluttered with coils of rope, paint cans, dusty stacks of magazines and newspapers. She found a chair, brushed it off and sat down, holding the bottle like a baby in her lap. Across the room was a water cooler. The rum she had consumed in the cab had helped, but it wasn't enough, not for both the physical and the mental hangovers.

She got up and went to the cooler. A grimy tumbler sat atop the upended water bottle and she rinsed it and poured it half full from the cooler. She took a long drink of the rum and chased it down with water. It was warm, room temperature, and it had a stale smell to it. Cleo felt beads of perspiration pop out on her forehead.

She squeezed her eyes shut and held her breath, trying desperately to will the drink to stay in her stomach. When she was finally certain it would, she opened her eyes and poured the rest of the water down the drain and capped the rum bottle.

Harry came in, accompanied by a short dark man whose smile seemed to spread from one ear to the other.

"All right, Cleo, everything's ready. Let's go."

"A fine boat, Señor Gregory!" the little man exulted. *"Muy bueno!* A bargain like you will never again find!"

"I've already bought it, Salazar, so save your sales pitch."

Salazar's smile did not fade, but he shrugged and turned away.

Harry took Cleo's arm, led her out of the building and across the yard toward the docks. A fresh breeze was blowing off the bay, rattling the fronds of two tall palms that stood at the end of the dock.

"She's the second boat there," Harry said as they went out onto the wooden dock. "That's it, the *Belle*."

Cleo stopped when they reached the stern of the boat. She knew very little about boats, but her impression was that this one was too small to venture out into the open ocean. "It—it isn't very big, is it?"

"She's not exactly a yacht, but she is sound and sea-worthy, and the engines are in excellent condition."

Cleo said sarcastically, "And you know all that from a five-minute inspection?"

"I know the broker who located her for me. I've bought boats through him before, and my Old Man did business with him. He's honest and he had a survey run on this boat before he recommended it. For the price, it was a good buy."

Cleo looked at him in surprise. "For the price? When did the price ever concern you?"

"Come on, get aboard," he said, hustling her down the dock and onto the boat. "Let's shove off; we've got a long way to go."

A quarter of an hour later the first heavy surge of the sea struck them as they reached the headland beneath the ruins of the fort. Not expecting the sudden shift, Cleo was thrown off balance and her drink slid across the top of the bulkhead, crashing against the binnacle.

"My God, Harry! Is this how it's going to be the rest of the way?"

"Afraid we'll run out of glasses? You can drink out of the bottle."

To reply would merely be to start an argument, so Cleo simply went below to the galley and re-made her drink. Before she came back, she experienced a slight pang of queasiness. She took a deep swallow of her drink, determined that she would not give in to seasickness. Harry would love to see her hanging over the rail. It would make him feel vastly superior.

"Look out there!" Harry said exultantly when she took the seat opposite him again. "Beautiful! Absolutely beautiful! Take a look, Cleo!"

She let her gaze go across the deep blue water to the shore of the island. She could make out a thin strip of white sand beyond the breakers, the lush green forest that came down to the sand, and the steep rise of the land beyond. Far inland, the mountains showed purple, hazy and majestic.

"How about it, Cleo? Would you swap this for the city? For snow and all those damned people?"

"In a minute!" she said flatly. But even as she said it —because it was expected of her—she knew that, somehow, she was caught up in all this abundant display of nature. There was a fascination about it, maybe even something a little atavistic. "What's this place like, the one we're going to?"

"St. Ursula? Don't tell me you're actually interested?"

"I think the word is 'resigned'," she said.

He turned back to the wheel, glancing at the compass. "I've never been there, but I suppose it's about the same as here. Water, sand, palm trees and shady-looking characters in baggy, white linen suits."

"Sounds great," Cleo said.

Harry grinned and flexed his hands on the wheel. "It's good to feel a boat under me again. You know, I was pretty good with boats before my old man died and I had to go to work. Dad had an old Wheeler he kept down at Sea Island. We used to spend the whole summer there, offshore fishing and cruising up and down the inland waterway. I could run a boat before I could drive a car." He looked at his wife. "Have you ever operated a boat like this one, Cleo?"

"Sure, Harry. Didn't I tell you? My dear father won a big yacht by saving the labels off whiskey bottles. Nobody else had half a chance."

"Poor but proud," Harry said, laughing. "Come here and let me show you how this thing works. You're going to have to spell me a little at the wheel before we get there."

"When will we get there?"

"It'll be sometime tomorrow morning."

Cleo picked up her glass, braced herself against the roll of the boat, and went across the cockpit to the helm for her lesson in the operation of the *Belle*.

CHAPTER THREE

S UNLIGHT STREAMED INTO the cabin, moving up and down on the clothes hammock alongside the bunk with each roll of the boat. Cleo stretched lazily after she awoke, idly watching the motion of the patch of light and listening to the steady sound of the engines.

The motion of the boat had lessened decidedly since she'd turned in sometime after midnight. From the angle of the sunlight she judged that it was still early. She was pleased that the state of her health was much improved from the previous morning, proving that a sea voyage had a salutary effect, or perhaps that rum was not as hangover-provoking as was gin and vermouth.

She got up and made her way down the companionway to the steps that led up to the deck. On the way she stopped at the galley and put water on to boil. She poked her head up through the companionway.

"Coffee?"

Harry nodded. "Just what I need. You did a pretty fair job of keeping us on course last night. We're right where I figured we ought to be. Should be in port in another couple of hours."

"I just did what you said—kept the compass on the number. Besides, I don't think you got much sleep sitting there in that deck chair."

She stepped back down into the galley. Through the opening she could see him sitting there at the wheel, poised, self-assured, in his element. In one of his elements. Harry had a variety of them. He was also a low seventies golfer, and a fine tennis player.

He had been brought up as a typical rich boy by a father who'd made it the hard way, and who wanted his only son to have all the things he'd missed.

The Old Man had died before Cleo met Harry, but over the years she had built up an image of him. Hard and ruthless in his relations with everyone but the boy, and making the mistake of never seeing far enough into the future to envision the boy without the father. The only thing that kept the chain of dry-goods stores together after the Old Man's death was the organization he had set up. The business could practically run itself, which was a very fortunate thing for Harry Gregory, who never bothered to learn in college the difference between a debit and a credit.

The water began to boil on the stove. Cleo spooned instant coffee into two cups and poured in the water. She handed Harry's cup up to him, then carried hers up and took her seat opposite the helm.

She looked around and saw the reason for the calmer seas. All about them were islands, small ones, large ones, some with strikingly white stretches of beach, others presenting fantastic rock formations against which the sea broke with a vengeance. To starboard she saw the patched gray sail of an inter-island sloop scudding before the morning breeze.

"The pristine beauty of dear old Mother Nature," she said.

"It's not a view you get from the Staten Island Ferry," Harry said. "How about cooking up something? There're eggs in the refrigerator, and some bacon."

"Aye, aye, Captain."

There was a ship's clock on the bulkhead at the forward end of the cabin. The time was five after seven. As she opened the refrigerator Cleo tried to remember how long it had been since she voluntarily got up at such an hour. Certainly not in all the years she had been married to Harry Gregory. She smiled, wondering if she would remember how to fry an egg.

Suddenly, she found herself facing the unimportant chore with something like anticipation, the delight of a small girl playing grown-up. Sophistication exacted its toll, removing the corny little thoughts the sophisticate cannot admit to.

The breakfast was good and Harry commented on it. "The sea agrees with you. The bacon's just right and the eggs are perfect."

"Just two of the little things that make life worth living," Cleo said. "Like Mom and apple pie and the corner drugstore." She hated herself for being cynical, especially since she didn't actually feel that way. She felt strangely and unreasonably hopeful. But she had reacted to Harry in the time-tested way. She had not forgotten what happened in the hotel and to strike back against his good humor, even in a small way, gave her a certain satisfaction.

The *Belle* entered the harbor at St. Ursula at nine o'clock. Far across the water from the entrance the town lay pink, buff and clean in the morning sun, a complete change from the bustling city they had left a day ago. No smokestacks marred the outline behind the quay and, looking at the peaceful island, Cleo had the fleeting sensation of having gone back somehow in time.

They crossed the broad bay and threaded through a thicket of anchored trading sloops to the gray stone quay that lined the harbor below the town.

A white schooner lay tied up alongside the quay ahead of them, obviously not a native boat, and yet, judging from its lack of fresh paint and the rusty streaks running down the topsides beneath the scuppers, not a luxury yacht either. The sails were furled. A man clad in tan shorts sat on the edge of the cabin trunk watching the *Belle* as it drew closer.

Harry eased up to the quay astern of the schooner and the man on the sailboat came back and took the lines. The boat secured, Harry stepped ashore.

"Thanks," he said to the stranger, turning back to help Cleo off the boat.

The man nodded. "You must be the folks who've rented the Carleton place."

Harry looked at him strangely. "How did you know that?"

"I can see you're not from a small town, Mr. Gregory."

"So you know who we are, as well."

He nodded. "I'm Casey Stribling. The *Antares* here is my boat." He indicated the white schooner.

"I see," said Harry. "Maybe you could tell me where I might find Mrs. Keever."

"Marla?" He turned and pointed across the broad, cobbled street. "That's her office right there, but it might be a little early for her."

"How about our boat? Will it be okay here?"

"For the time being," Stribling said. "You might want to keep her anchored down at the east end of the harbor, though. There's a shop and a marine railway down there, and most of the time there's somebody around who can sort of keep an eye on things."

"Well, thanks, Stribling," Harry said, taking Cleo's arm again.

"Any time," Casey Stribling said. He was looking at Cleo, his eyes twinkling. "Any time at all."

They crossed the street to the building and stopped before a door marked: *Marla Keever. Real Estate. Public Stenographer. Notary Public.* The small office was situated between a bar on one side and a dry-goods store on the other.

"Maybe she takes in washing, too," observed Cleo.

The door was open and they stepped inside. The office was not a great deal larger than a phone booth. There were two chairs against one wall, and opposite the door was a desk. Behind the desk sat a woman, asleep, her feet propped up on the desk before her. Her skirt had slipped up to her hips, exposing long, shapely, well-tanned thighs, and the edge of white panties.

"I don't think I've ever seen a real estate agent from quite this angle before," Cleo said.

The sound of the voice woke the woman. Her eyes opened sleepily and she stared at the two people before her.

"The Gregorys?" she asked.

"That's right," said Harry. "You must be Mrs. Keever."

She dropped her feet to the floor and stood up, arranging her skirt without embarrassment or self-consciousness. "Call me Marla. Everybody else does."

She was of medium height, full-bodied, and it was obvious that the large, roundish breasts pushing against her blouse were not restrained by a brassiere. Cleo judged her to be in her late thirties or early forties.

"By the way," Harry said, "is it the custom here to let everybody on the island know everything that's going on?"

Marla Keever gave him a puzzled look as he went on.

"A fellow met us at the quay and it turned out he knew exactly who we were, where we were going to stay, and God knows what else about us."

"Oh!" Marla said, brightening. "That must have been Casey."

"That's right."

"Your letters didn't mention that your coming here was supposed to be a secret. If you'd wanted to keep it quiet, you should have told me so. I'm a loudmouth by nature, but I can keep a secret. Besides, you won't be here half an hour before everybody on the island knows all about you, so what's the difference?"

Cleo smiled at the candid answer to Harry's question, but Harry saw no humor in it.

"We'd like to see the house now," he said.

"Sure thing." She walked around them to the door. "My car's broken down. We'll take the taxi."

At the door she put two fingers in her mouth and gave out with a shrill whistle. A few seconds later an aged Ford station wagon pulled up outside.

The driver was a huge man of indeterminate age, with a face that had all the appearance of having been hammered in with a battering ram.

"Wh-wh-where to, Marla?" he asked.

"The Carleton place up on the ridge, Tiger. Folks, meet Tiger Mobley, ex-heavyweight contender. Tiger, this is Mr. and Mrs. Gregory."

"P-p-pleased to meetcha," he said.

"Pull over there to that boat and we'll get our luggage," Harry told him.

Marla Keever kept up a running conversation as they drove up into the low hills to the house. The roadway sloped gently up from the town, through thick stands of logwood, mahogany, tall palms, and huge flowering shrubs of many kinds, varicolored and exotically beautiful. At the top of the ridge Tiger turned off onto a white drive and pulled to a stop before a house. It was a rambling, one-story structure, pale pink with a red tile roof that sparkled in the bright sunlight.

"Well, this is it," Marla said. "You know, you got a very good deal on this place."

Tiger jumped out and opened the car doors for them. "Yeah," he said, "this here's a real nice house."

Marla led the way into the house and Tiger followed, bringing the luggage. He stayed close to Cleo, watching her with an almost childlike fascination.

The house was large, with high ceilings and a great many windows. "I hope you're not expecting me to do the housekeeping," Cleo said to her husband.

Harry turned toward Marla. "Did you make arrangements for a servant as I asked you to?"

"I've got an Indian woman lined up, but she can't come until tomorrow. I also arranged for a car. It'll be ready about noon."

"I—I got to finish fixing the distributor," Tiger grinned.

"Tiger's the best mechanic on the island," Marla said, adding, "Among his other accomplishments."

Cleo smiled at the big man. "I'll bet you were a good boxer, too."

His reaction was that of a lonesome dog that has been patted on the head. "I—I woulda won the champeenship if I hadn'ta had this here accident."

Cleo wanted to ask him about the accident, but Marla led them through the house to a broad patio. Cleo walked across to a low stone wall. A hundred feet below, accessible by stairs, was a crescent-shaped beach. The sea was green at the edge and becoming a deep blue as the bottom shelved steeply away from the shore into the depths.

"I think the place will do nicely," Harry said. "I'm going back down to the village to see about the boat, Cleo. Do you want to go along and pick up some groceries?"

Cleo turned and put her hand on Tiger's arm. "I'll bet if I gave Tiger a list he'd do it for me."

His battered face split into a grin. "S-sure I would! And I'd do it good, too!"

"You've got to finish fixing the car," Marla reminded him.

He frowned deeply, as if some catastrophe had taken place. Then he brightened again. "Soon as I finish the car!"

Harry was saying, "You've already got my check for two weeks' rental, Marla. My—my guests are coming in on the fifteenth, and I ought to be able to tell you definitely then how long we'll want the place."

Cleo's eyes popped wide. "Do you mean we might be stuck down here longer than two *weeks*? I won't do it Harry! I positively won't—"

Harry took her arm firmly. "We'll discuss it later, Cleo."

"Later, hell! We'll—"

Harry's fingers bit into her flesh. "Later, dear? Now get your list made out and we'll be on our way."

Cleo opened her mouth to protest further but Harry's hand tightened again on her arm and she nodded agreement. She made out a brief list and handed it to Tiger.

"I'll be back as soon as the car's ready," Harry said. Turning to Marla he added, "Let's go."

When their car, a Volkswagen, arrived Harry and Cleo drove down to the village that evening and had dinner in the hotel. There were hardly half a dozen others in the dining room, and the waiter assured them that business was unusually slow, but would be much better when the cruise ship stopped off later in the month.

A steady rain began to fall as they drove back up the ridge later. At the house, Cleo stood at the open patio door and listened to the heavy downpour. Then, as quickly as it had begun, the rain stopped. But, for a long time, the water continued to drip noisily down from the trees.

"Harry?"

"Yes?"

The dripping of the rain water was lessening, and Cleo could now hear the heavy sound of the breakers below on the beach. "Harry, who is Freeman?"

"Who is—?" She heard him get up from his chair and start across the room behind her. "Where did you get that name?"

She shrugged. "I don't know. Maybe I heard you mention it."

"You didn't hear me mention it."

"What difference does it make where I heard it?" She turned around. He was standing close to her, an odd expression on his face. "Are you going to tell me who he is?" she asked.

"I went to college with a fellow by that name."

"Aha! So this is a school reunion! And Heinrich, is he another old school chum?"

Harry grabbed her roughly, his face twisted with anger. "All right, Cleo! Where the hell did you pick up those names?"

"You're hurting me, Harry." He released her and she went on. "As a spy, darling, they'd have you against the wall in five minutes. I got the names off your cablegram." She gave a little laugh of amusement. "You should have torn it into little pieces and eaten it."

Harry was not amused. "That's why we came down here, to meet them. Now don't ask any more questions, Cleo. The less you know about this thing right now, the better. If anybody starts asking any questions, just tell them we're down here on a holiday. Do you understand?"

"If you say so, Harry."

She turned and stared back out at the night. She did not really care what Harry was up to. She listened to the dripping of the rain and the steady booming of the surf, thinking how nice it would be to be back in the city, in the stale, smoky, almost unbreathable air of a club, surrounded by noise of people having fun. Idly, she thought of Johnny Crawford and wondered if Harry had really checked up on her or had merely made some smart guesses. As for Johnny, he meant nothing to her. He had been male, handy and discreet.

She leaned against the doorway and rubbed her hands together. Maybe Harry was right, maybe there was a touch of nympho in her. Suddenly, unbidden, the image of a man came into her mind. It was the man on the sailboat, the man named Casey Stribling. He wore no shirt and his chest and shoulders were deep bronze, gleaming. He was looking directly at her, and he was smiling.

CHAPTER FOUR

O N THE AFTERNOON of the fifteenth the mailboat pulled into the harbor at St. Ursula. It was hardly an imposing sight to Cleo as she stood on the quay with Harry, awaiting the arrival of their guests. The boat was high-sided and stubby, and had the appearance of antiquity.

A small crowd had gathered at the quayside as the vessel came alongside. An unintelligible order was shouted from the wheelhouse, muffled bells rang belowdecks, and crewmen fore and aft threw lines to waiting hands ashore. The mail boat had arrived.

"I see Freeman!" Harry said, pushing forward toward the gangway that had been placed at the rail of the boat. "Gene! Gene! Hi!"

The man who responded to the call stood at the rail. He was fairly tall, with the soft appearance of a man who does not live by physical effort. The breeze blew his thinning hair and, as he grinned down at Harry it seemed to Cleo that the smile he offered belonged on a salesman coming to see a prospect, rather than on a friend coming to visit an old friend.

Seconds later he came ashore, ushering a thin old man before him. His hand was outthrust at Harry, and the two shook hands heartily, as was to be expected of classmates who had not seen each other for a long time. Almost immediately, however, Freeman's attention was fixed on Cleo.

"My wife Cleo," Harry said, by way of introduction. "Cleo, this is Gene Freeman."

A toothy smile spread over Freeman's face. "You always had good taste, Harry. And good luck." He turned and took hold of the old man's arm. "Well, here he is. Meet Max Heinrich."

The old man's eyes stared as if seeing nothing. Freeman shook him. "Hey, Max! Where's your manners? *Achtung*, old buddy!"

"For Christ's sake, Gene," Harry whispered quickly. "Watch what you say. Come on, get him over to the car and let's get back to the house."

"How about the luggage?"

"Luggage? All right, you get it. I'll take him to the car and wait for you there."

Harry moved away quickly, steering the old man toward the car. Cleo watched them go, then turned to Freeman. "Very touching reunion. Actually heart-warming."

Freeman gave her a puzzled look. Cleo twirled her handbag and shook her head. "No, he hasn't told me what this is all about."

He looked past her to the car, then pursed his lips. "You're really his wife?"

"What the hell do you think I am?"

"Hey!" he said, laughing, "don't blow your top! Just asking."

"Yes, I really am his wife."

"I see." He looked back toward the boat, where a deck hand was bringing two suitcases down the gangway. "There's our stuff."

"Traveling light."

"There are times when one has to."

"Did you smuggle the old man out of Germany or something like that? Is he some kind of criminal?"

Freeman laughed. "Ask Harry."

"I did, but Harry acts as though he's been taking a correspondence course on how to become a member of the CIA."

"I like a woman with a sense of humor!" Freeman said heartily. He stopped before the man with the luggage, looking at Cleo in frank appraisal. His gaze dropped slowly from her face to her breasts, then down until it reached her feet. He looked back into her eyes, shaking his head. "All this *and* a sense of humor?"

Harry drove nervously going back, the same as he had coming down earlier. Once he had to slam on the brakes to avoid running over a pair of goats being driven through the streets by a native woman.

"The goddamn idiots! There ought to be some law—"

"Just take it easy, Harry," Freeman said. "Don't want anything to foul up now, do we? Besides, we wouldn't want to shake Max up."

Harry glanced quickly over his shoulder at the two men sitting in the rear seat. He went on, his driving improving noticeably.

At the house, Heinrich paused as he got out of the car and, for the first time since getting off the boat, seemed to take some interest in his surroundings. "A very nice place," he said slowly. He looked at Cleo and smiled thinly. "Yes, a very good place for an old man. A tired old man."

She regarded him closely for the first time. His age was impossible to guess. The thin, bent, sickly body belied the occasional flicker of his pale gray eyes. His hair was wispy and white, and when he spoke it was apparent that many teeth were missing.

"I am looking forward to my stay," he said politely.

As they walked to the door Freeman said, "Anything you want, Max baby! Anything at all! Right, Harry?"

They went into the house and Freeman put the bags down. Heinrich turned to him. "I believe I would like something to drink, Gene. Brandy, if there is any."

"Got any brandy, Harry?"

"I think so. Cleo, would you see about it?"

"Also, Gene," Heinrich said, "my sweater is there in the valise. I am a little cold."

"I'll take him out on the patio, into the sun," Harry said quickly. "It's nice and warm out there. Hurry up with the brandy, Cleo."

Harry helped the old man out to the patio and seated him in a reclining chair. Cleo went to the makeshift bar in the next room and found a bottle of cognac. Freeman started to open Heinrich's suitcase, but he came and stood behind Cleo.

"How come you came along on this little jaunt?" he asked.

Cleo shrugged. "Harry wanted me to, so here I am."

"You don't like it, do you? I can tell. You've got city written all over you, baby."

She had just tilted to the cognac bottle to pour the drink when she felt Freeman's hands on her waist. She paused, his hands moving slowly across her belly and clasping in front of her.

"Yes, ma'am, you are definitely not the out-islands type."

"Gene?" Cleo said, slowly putting the bottle down on the table.

"Yeah, baby?" he whispered in her ear.

In spite of herself, she did not want to break the contact, but neither did she want Harry to come in unexpectedly to find them this way. Freeman's hands moved again, up until they touched against the lower part of her breasts.

"Gene," she said softly, "if you don't get your hot little hands off me, and damned well right now, then I am going to turn around and give you a knee right in the—right where it'll do the most good. Do you understand me?"

For a moment he was thrown off balance by the gentle, seductive tone of her voice, and then he laughed and jerked his hands away. "Loud and clear, lady!" He tapped her smartly on the buttock and stepped back. "Loud and clear!"

"And that means from now on, is that loud and clear, too?"

"Oh, sure!" he said. He opened Heinrich's bag and found the sweater. "I like the way you handled that, Cleo. That was good, and it told me a couple of things about you."

Cleo poured the brandy.

"First thing is, you're no prude." Freeman went on. "If you were, you wouldn't have let me touch you. The second thing was that you really wanted me to do that, but you were afraid of Harry. Otherwise, you would have raised hell."

"Very analytic. Here, take this tray out." She put the bottle of cognac and ice bowl on a tray.

"Analytic or not, I do know women. And I know Harry. I know Harry's not man enough to keep you content." He slung the sweater over his shoulder and picked up the tray. "I'll give you notice, Cleo. Fair warning. I'm going to get into those well-filled little pants of yours before this junket's done."

"Brother! An egomaniac!"

He started out with the tray, then he stopped and said, "There're all kinds of maniacs."

Heinrich accepted his brandy gratefully, and quickly had two more. "It was a long journey, eh, Gene?" he said at length. "But you are still a young man, and such a journey does not tire you."

"You used to do a lot more traveling in the old days, Max."

The old man grinned. "Ah yes, but as you say, that was the old days!" He finished his brandy and looked at Cleo. "Would you be so kind as to show me to my room, Frau Gregory? I believe I shall take a nap."

When she had taken the old man to his room and returned to the patio. Harry and Freeman were in heated discussion.

"I say we start the first thing tomorrow morning!" Harry said.

Freeman poured cognac into a glass. "Harry, you've got to remember the old boy was in a Russian prison for one hell of a long time. He's old and sick. We've got to go easy with him."

"Russian prison?" Cleo said. "Heinrich? Who is he, Harry? What is he doing here?"

"That's none of your concern, Cleo," he snapped. "Keep out of it."

"Why not tell her, Harry?" Freeman said. He smiled at Cleo. "You know how women are. Curious. She'll find out sooner or later—a little here, a little there. She might as well have the straight story."

Harry Gregory frowned and pushed one hand through his hair in a quick motion. "The more people who know—" he started to say, shrugging his shoulders and picking up the cognac bottle. "What the hell," he continued, pouring himself a drink, "I suppose you're right."

Freeman walked to the edge of the patio and sat down on the stone wall. "Our friend Max is a German, Cleo."

"I figured that much."

"I met him in Germany about six weeks ago. I was working for an automobile importing outfit, and one day I was in a little joint having a beer, jawing with the guy behind the bar, and this old guy sits down beside me and asks me if I'm an American.

"Well, at first I thought he was just some bum cadging drinks, and I started to give him the brush. But," he continued, smiling broadly, "being a good-natured fellow, I told the bartender to set the old man up a brew.

"The old guy accepted the beer, but he told me that wasn't the reason he wanted to talk to me. We went to a table and he started talking.

"At first I thought it was Some kind of a joke, and then I thought maybe the old boy was off his rocker. But the more he talked, the harder I began to listen. Maybe it was the way he talked, or the way he looked, I don't really know."

Freeman stopped for a moment, looking out at the sea and the distant islands.

"He started talking about money," he went on. "Lots of money. He asked me if I would be interested, and I said it depended on what I had to do. He told me all we had to do was go dig it up, that was all." Freeman laughed. "Well, I figured then that one of my ideas had been right, after all. The guy was some kind of a nut. I finished my beer and told the old man to drink up and to save his yarn for the tourists.

"But Max wouldn't give up. He said the only reason he was telling me about it was that he couldn't handle it alone. The Russians had just turned him loose. He'd been in a POW camp there since back in the war, and when he came home there wasn't any home. There was nothing and nobody to come back to. He had no property, no money. On top of that, he was sick.

"I started to get up and walk out right then, but I didn't. I ordered us a couple more beers, and Max went on with his story. He had been a U-boat officer during the war, something like an executive officer, just beneath the skipper. They had a mission to pick up a particular item at a secret South American rendezvous and make delivery to Nazi agents in the States. On the way up, the captain took Max aside for a little talk. It seems that the two of them agreed on one thing: Germany was losing the war. So this captain told Max what was in the package they were to deliver."

"Money?" Cleo asked.

Freeman nodded. "He said he didn't see why the money had to be delivered at all, that it would be the same as throwing it away. He suggested to Max that they could stop off, hide the dough and go back after the war and pick it up. Max agreed. They'd pull a little double cross on Hitler and—"

"Not precisely what you call a double cross, Herr Freeman."

They all turned and saw Heinrich standing in the doorway, wearing a robe and slippers, his thin hair awry.

"I could not sleep so I came to get another glass of brandy, if that is permissible, Frau Gregory?"

"Permissible?" Freeman said, hurriedly picking up glass and bottle and walking toward the old man. "Max baby, like I said, you name it and it's yours! "

Cleo looked at her husband. "Harry, do you mean to tell me we're down here on some half-cocked treasure hunt? Do you actually *believe* this insane story? It's—"

"Shut up, Cleo," Harry said.

"I knew you were gullible, but not *this* gullible!"

"I said for you to shut your mouth!"

"And because of this—this pipe dream I'm down here on this lousy island when I could be home—"

Harry swung hard, his open hand catching her flush across the cheek and sending her sprawling.

"Herr Gregory," the old man said. "No. Please do not blame your wife. She is right—"

"She's *right?*" Harry exploded. "What the hell does that mean?"

"I mean she cannot help becoming—what is the word?—skeptical."

Cleo slowly rubbed the side of her face. "You're damned right I'm skeptical! I think you've taken these two idiots in."

Heinrich smiled faintly. "We shall see, Frau Gregory. We shall see."

"It—it just doesn't make sense," she insisted.

"Listen to the whole thing, Cleo," said Gene Freeman. "It might not add up any better after you've heard it, but at least hear it out."

Cleo looked around at the three men and then sat down docilely.

The old man spoke. "Reiner, that was the name of the *Kapitan* of my boat. Reiner surfaced the boat three nights after our talk, and I went ashore in the inflatable raft, along with two seamen and the money. I had no idea where we were. That had been our plan. Reiner was to know where we were, and I was to know the precise location of the cache ashore."

Heinrich smiled and sipped his brandy. "It is universal that conspirators never trust one another, eh? So it was done—I marked the place. The seamen knew nothing of what we were doing, and we returned to the submarine."

"No one questioned your stopping this way?" Cleo said.

"*Liebchen,*" said the old man with a shake of his head, "aboard the *Unterseeboot* there are no questions. It is a world in itself, a microcosm, and the *Kapitan* is the deity. No, there were no questions."

"Where is the captain now?"

"He is dead. It was our intention to surrender ourselves to the Americans as soon as possible. We continued to the north, and entered the Atlantic convoy lanes. The second day, ships were sighted and Reiner ordered the boat to the surface. But something went wrong. We were attempting to surrender, but a destroyer began firing on us. The sea was rough and the day was growing foggy, even so they scored a hit and the U-boat began to sink.

"I managed to launch a small life raft and I pulled Reiner aboard with me. By this time the fog had settled heavily over the whole sea. We were soon out of sight of other survivors, though we could hear them calling. We drifted for several hours, hearing ships all about us. Reiner was badly hurt and needed medical attention.

"Late in the day the fog lifted and we were picked up by a freighter of the convoy, our rescuers perhaps thinking we were survivors of some ship that had been torpedoed. But it was too late to help Reiner, and he died shortly after we were taken aboard the ship. When he seemed certain there was no hope for him, he told me the name of the group of islands where we had stopped."

"But—but that must have been at least sixteen years ago," Cleo said.

Heinrich nodded. "Yes."

"You were in a Russian prison?"

Again he nodded. "This freighter was an American ship. When it was determined that I was a German officer, many wanted to throw me back into the sea." He smiled. "I cannot say I blamed them. I couldn't blame them at all. At any rate, the convoy went on to its destination, Murmansk, Russia. I was turned over to the Russians and that was all there was to it. The Russians kept many Germans long after the end of the war. There are many who are still there."

Cleo sat quietly for a moment, trying to assimilate all of it. Then she said, "How did Harry get involved in this?"

Freeman answered her question. "A thing like this takes capital, Cleo. Max was flat, of course, and all I could scratch up was a few hundred dollars. So I got in touch with Harry. In fact, I put Max up in a hotel and flew back to the States to give Harry the whole story."

"And gullible me, I bought it," Harry said.

Cleo shook her head. "I—I just can't believe it. I can't—" She turned and looked intently at Heinrich. "How much money is there supposed to be?"

The old man lifted his brandy glass and turned it slowly in both hands. "Who is to say?"

"You must have some idea. How much?"

He pursed his lips. "A great deal. Perhaps *Zwei Million*—"

"I don't understand German."

"Two million dollars, American. Perhaps more, who knows?"

The words dropped like a quiet bomb amidst the little group on the patio. The old man nodded and smiled. "A great deal of money, yes? Perhaps we should drink a toast to good luck." He pulled himself erect and lifted his glass. *"Prosit!"* He turned the glass up and drank off his brandy.

CHAPTER FIVE

RENE, the Indian servant Marla Keever had hired, appeared at the door to the patio.

"A telephone call for you, Mr. Gregory," she said.

Harry was standing beside a table on which were spread a number of charts. Heinrich sat before the table in a rattan chair, his thin hands before him on the charts. Freeman was to his right, leaning forward intently.

"I'll be right there," Harry said to the servant. He bent over the charts. "Can't you narrow it down, Max? There are one hell of a lot of islands in this group."

The old man smiled ruefully and made a gesture of helplessness with his hands. "I am fortunate to know as much as I do, Harry. There was a beach and it was on the north shore of the island. I took note of the pole star, but there was no other way—"

"Allright, allright," Harry said tightly. He straightened and walked into the house.

Cleo came across the patio and stopped beside the old man. She wore a two-piece bathing suit, a bikini, and Freeman looked at her in frank admiration.

"If this thing really exists, Max," she said, "do you honestly think you've got a chance of finding it?"

"You ought to tell us how you marked the cache," Freeman put in, glancing at Heinrich. "That way we could split up—"

Heinrich touched Freeman's arm and smiled at him. "Yes, and perhaps in that way you could avoid giving an old man his share when the money was found?"

Freeman gave him a pained look. "Max! You don't *trust* me?"

The German laughed silently and shook his head. "Let us simply say that it is nothing personal, eh?"

It brought a laugh from Cleo. She ran one hand through her red hair and turned toward Freeman. "Max may not be well, Gene, but he's certainly not stupid."

Harry came out from the house. "That was Vansant over at the boat dock. He's found a skiff that'll serve as a dinghy, which means the equipment is all set." He walked to the table and looked at the old man. "How about it, Max? You've been here two days now; you ought to be rested from your trip. Are you ready to get moving?"

Heinrich nodded. He reached for the glass of brandy before him. "I am ready when you are, Harry."

"The sooner the better!" Freeman said, rubbing his hands together.

"Then we start tomorrow morning," Harry said, his excitement showing in his face. He lifted his arm and looked at his watch. "It's four o'clock now. Cleo, you take the car and run down to the village. We've already got all the canned stuff we'll need aboard the boat. Get some fresh vegetables, meat, anything you think we might need for the first few days. You might get a few quarts of milk for Max."

"Milk?" Cleo said, her eyebrows lifting. "What for? His hangovers?"

Harry's eyes narrowed and a muscle twitched in his jaw. "I've had about enough of your wry humor, Cleo. Now you get in the goddamn car and do what I said. I'll call Vansant back and have him put ice aboard. You take the stuff to the dock and leave it with him."

She started to say something, but Harry had turned his attention back to the charts and was speaking to Heinrich. She caught Freeman's look of amusement as she walked into the house.

The three men were still on the patio, deep in concentration over the charts, when Cleo got into the little car and headed toward the village.

The afternoon sun slanted down from behind her, gleaming off the town below and the harbor beyond. There was something about this place that was getting to her, in a way she never would have believed possible. A vague contentment seemed to pervade her, a feeling that this was something she had been missing for a long time. It seemed to put aside all the strife she had known these past nine years with Harry.

She drove through the village to the quayside market where she had been doing her shopping. A breeze came in off the harbor, bringing with it the smell of the fishing boats that had come in during the day.

When she finished with the shopping and had the groceries and supplies loaded into the Volkswagen, Cleo walked down to the quay to watch the boats. Beyond the anchored fishing boats a white schooner ghosted across the harbor.

"That's—that's Cap'n Casey." a voice said close by.

Cleo looked around. Tiger Mobley had walked up behind her, unheard, and was gazing out at the schooner.

"Hello, Tiger."

He touched the bill of his cap with a huge hand and grinned. "He-hello, Miss Cleo."

"Is he coming in from a trip someplace?"

"Huh?"

"Captain Stribling," she said, pointing toward the schooner.

"Oh. He takes out some of them p-people from the hotel."

"I see." Cleo ran her hand through her hair, feeling the caress of the breeze on her face. Suddenly, she had a strong desire to be out there aboard the schooner. There was a strange attraction in a man like Stribling. She had known that since the first day when he had helped them tie up the *Belle.* She smiled at Mobley. "I've got to be going."

"Can I—can I take you someplace in my cab?"

"No, thank you. I've got the car."

"I wouldn't—wouldn't charge you nothin'," he said quickly.

"How can you make a living with your cab if you don't charge?" she asked, her eyes twinkling with amusement.

He shrugged his massive shoulders and the battered face wrinkled into a frown. "I'll m-make it up on some of them tourists up at the hotel."

"Maybe some other time, Tiger." She gave him another smile and walked away.

A half an hour later, having delivered the supplies to Vansant, Cleo pulled up before the house.

An early morning mist hung over the waters of the harbor as the *Belle* pulled away from the dock. Cleo stood in the cockpit with a coffee cup in her hand. She had tried to talk Harry into letting her stay in St. Ursula while the three men went on the hunt, but he had insisted on her coming along. "We need a coook," he'd said. "And you can help look after the old man."

So here she was, stuck, except that for some strange reason her feeling of resentment had left her. She looked at Heinrich sitting in a deck chair with his eyes closed. Already there was a glass clutched in his hands, just as it had been almost continuously since his arrival. Freeman stood beside Harry at the wheel, holding a folded chart. They reminded Cleo of two greedy little boys setting out to rob a candy store.

"Cleo."

She turned and saw that it was Heinrich who had spoken to her. He was looking at her, his gray eyes pale and slightly bloodshot. A faint smile was on his thin lips.

"What is it, Max? What do you want?"

"Oh, I do not want anything. Come sit beside me." He reached out and touched the chair next to him.

Cleo sat down. Her attitude toward Max had begun to change, too. She felt pity toward him now, about his long imprisonment and his poor health, and the way he seemed to be completely alone in the world.

"I am sorry that Harry made you come along," the old man said. "In a way, it is my fault."

She shook her head and sipped her coffee. "Don't let it worry you."

"But it does worry me. A pretty woman like you should not be made to accompany an old man and two—" He stopped abruptly and looked toward Harry and Freeman.

"Two what?" Cleo prodded him.

Heinrich shrugged and took a drink of his brandy. "I should not be one to find fault. Without them I would not be here. Nevertheless, I feel to blame that you are not where you want to be."

"Where do you think I want to be, Max?"

"Somewhere. You do not like the islands, though I suspect your feelings have changed somewhat since coming here."

She looked at him in surprise. "I'd say you are something of an observer."

"I know that you are not happy."

Cleo finished her coffee. "It's too early in the morning for philosophizing." She looked toward the town that lay stretched along the western side of the harbor. The sun had just reached the crest of the hills opposite the town, and the bright sunlight moved across the rooftops as if trying to wake the town for some occasion.

"It's beautiful, isn't it?" Cleo said. She took a cigarette from her blouse pocket and lit it. She took a deep drag and looked back at Heinrich. "Did you sink a great many ships?"

"Did I—" Then, comprehending, he nodded. "Yes. We sank a great many. We killed many brave men. We made many orphans and widows."

"Harry was in the navy."

"He handles the boat well."

As if knowing they were talking about him, Harry turned. "How about some coffee, Cleo?"

She got up and went below to the galley. Freeman stuck his head in the companionway. "Make it two, okay?"

Cleo nodded and took down the mugs. She spooned in instant mix and poured the hot water. Through the window above the galley stove she saw that they had reached the narrow passage at the mouth of the harbor, and the boat was beginning to swing eastward.

As the boat cleared the harbor, it took on the familiar roll she had grown accustomed to on the trip to St. Ursula. The coffee mugs slid across the counter top on a particularly heavy roll and Cleo grabbed them.

Someone touched her shoulder. She looked around into Gene Freeman's grinning face.

"I thought you might need a hand down here," he said.

"If there's something you've got," she said, "it's hands. Here." She held out one mug to him.

Freeman's smile faded only slightly. "Look if we got off to a bad start, what do you say we begin again."

Cleo pursed her lips and tilted her head. "And just where would you want to start?"

Freeman's eyes twinkled and he tasted his coffee. "I believe in supply and demand. Been a salesman all my life and I know it works. Now, I happen to know you're doing without a commodity that I can supply."

She couldn't hold back a smile. "You've got gall, Gene. Unless I'm way off, you're propositioning me. This boat is forty-two feet long. My husband is here, not to mention Max. Just where do you think such a consummation could take place? And even if you had an answer for that, what in hell makes you think I'm the least bit interested in you?"

"Opportunity is never lacking if you keep your eyes open," he said. "We'll be stopping quite a bit. Lots of islands. Lots of opportunity."

"If you go in for rape," Cleo said.

He chuckled and turned to go topside. He looked back briefly. "We'll see. We'll see."

"You egotistical—"

But he was gone, and Cleo paused a moment, wondering if she was going to have trouble with him. Then she picked up Harry's coffee and followed Freeman out onto the deck.

For an hour the *Belle* headed east through the chain of islands. Freeman spelled Harry at the wheel and Harry sat down with Heinrich and Cleo.

"Where are we going?" Cleo asked him. "Why don't we stop and start looking for this buried treasure?" She waved her hand around at the islands that lay all about them.

Harry shook his head. "That's a woman for you. No organization."

"So I'm unorganized. But why do we keep going?"

"We decided to start at the easternmost part of the islands and work west. That way we won't miss any of them. Also, that way we start a good distance from St. Ursula. Any curiosity we might arouse will have a chance to die down. Now, does that answer your question?"

"I suppose so."

Harry put his hand on Heinrich's arm. "How do you feel, Max? This shouldn't bother an old salt like you."

"Being an old salt is no help. I've known men who were seamen all their lives, and yet always became sick the first day out of port. However, I feel fine. Perhaps a bit more brandy?" He held out his glass.

"Cleo," Harry said, nodding at Heinrich's empty glass.

She got up and moved toward the companionway. *Cook, nursemaid, bartender...*

As she passed Freeman she felt a sudden twinge on her buttock. Freeman grinned as he drew back his hand.

Cleo stopped and glared at him. She rubbed her bottom. "You do that again, Freeman, and I'll show you a couple of tricks I know. Believe me, you won't like them."

The hands of the clock on the bulkhead stood at a few minutes past eleven when they reached the last of the islands.

Ahead of the boat lay open water, clear to the horizon. Far to the southeast, great banks of white cumulus clouds hung over the water, shining in the bright sunlight. Twenty yards ahead of the *Belle*, a school of flying fish broke the surface, skimming between the waves.

"This is where we begin," Harry said, easing back on the throttles and picking up the folded chart from atop the bulkhead. He turned on the pilot seat. "Max! Wake him up, Cleo."

The old man was slumped in the deck chair, the glass overturned in his lap and the remains of his last drink spilled across the leg of his trousers. Cleo put her hand on his shoulder and shook him gently. Heinrich mumbled something in German and Cleo shook him again.

His eyes popped open. *"Eh! Eh!"*

"Wake up, Max," she said. "Harry wants you."

The German looked around and saw that the boat had stopped. He got to his feet slowly, shaking off Cleo's effort to help, and made his way to the helm, rubbing his hand through his thin, wispy hair. "We begin?" he asked Harry.

Freeman pointed to the islands which lay several hundred yards to the south. "There's a beach right there."

Heinrich glanced at the compass, then at the small island. Against the eastern end the seas broke heavily before the trade wind, but the north shore presented a calm aspect, lying as it did somewhat in the lee of the island.

"We will begin there, Harry," the old man said. His eyes went to the chart and a bony finger settled on the paper. "This is the one. Here."

Several minutes later the anchor went down in three fathoms of crystal water. Two hundred feet away, waves broke smoothly on a white, palm-fringed beach.

"I think we can run the skiff ashore without any trouble," Harry said. He turned to Cleo. "Want to go ashore?"

She started to decline, but the trip on the boat had been monotonous, and she decided it would be good to stretch. "Allright."

Freeman pulled the skiff alongside and hung the boarding ladder in position. He climbed down into the small boat.

"Okay, Max. Come on, I'll give you a hand."

Heinrich got into the boat and Cleo and Harry followed. With Harry at the oars, a few moments later, the boat rode in on the back of a wave and skidded to a halt on the coarse sand of the beach.

"Everybody out!" Harry called, leaping over the side. Together, they pulled the boat clear of the water and made the painter secure to the trunk of a palm.

"Where to, Max?" Freeman asked, his anticipation edging his voice. "I still say that if you'd tell us just how you marked this thing, we might be able to cut down the time it's liable to take."

"Thank you again for your consideration, Gene," the German said with a grin. "But I shall let you know when we locate the marker. Did you bring along the machete?"

Freeman reached into the skiff and lifted the long-bladed knife. "Right here."

"Then I think we should start at the end of this beach and work toward the west."

The beach ended several yards back from the breakers, the land rising to a height of some ten feet into a dense thicket of palms and other tropical growth.

Max moved down the beach, the others following. Cleo sensed the rising excitement in the others. She felt it herself, a feeling of adventure, the reaching of the end of a rainbow.

They reached the eastern tip of the island. The gently sloping white sand met an abutment of rock that rose abruptly from the breaking seas. Max paused, looked around at his companions, then pushed aside the foliage at the edge of the beach and began his trek to the west, paralleling the beach.

It proved slow going, very slow indeed. Freeman's patience wore thin after the first half hour.

"For Christ's sake, Max! It'll take us a hundred years to search all the beaches in these islands at this rate! Let's speed this up!"

The old man stopped and sat down on the trunk of a fallen sapodilla. "The marker could be obscured by the brush after all this time, Gene." He reached into his pocket and produced a half pint bottle, which he uncorked and turned up to his mouth. He took two swallows, his Adam's apple bobbing quickly under the parchment-like flesh of his throat. He wiped his mouth on the back of his hand. "We would not want to miss it and have to go all over this again, now would we?"

"You can trust us, Max!" Freeman spread his hands, doubtless to show his honesty. "Tell us how it's marked, then I can start looking at the other end of the damned island—"

Heinrich's head shook slowly but firmly. "I have only one piece of insurance, my friend. This is it." He tapped his skull with his forefinger.

"Let's get moving," Harry said.

By midafternoon the entire north shore of the little island had been thoroughly searched, without results.

Max stretched out on his bunk aboard the *Belle* as the island was checked off on the chart and an anchorage made at the second island. There was a long curved beach along the north shore. The anchor was dropped.

"Wake the old man up, Cleo," Harry said.

She went below and shook Max by the shoulder. He opened his eyes and smiled weakly up at her.

"You don't feel like any more today, do you?" she wanted to know.

"Perhaps it was the sun." He strained to raise himself on the bunk, and Cleo slid her arm beneath him to help him up. "Would you get a bit of brandy for me, *Liebchen?*"

"Maybe it's the brandy that's getting you."

He shook his head. "I would not have gotten this far without it. Please?"

"What's holding you up down there!" Freeman yelled down the companionway.

"Just hold your horses!" Cleo yelled back. She poured the brandy and handed it to the old man, watching him drink it.

He nodded when he was done. "That is better!"

They went ashore again. The terrain was rougher than before, with many wind-felled trees and jagged outcroppings of rock. Once, the German lost his footing and if Harry had not caught him he would have gone down a fifteen-foot drop to rocks below.

"We rest awhile," Max said, thanking Harry. "I—I am afraid I am not quite up to this. It will take a day or two—"

"You goddamn stubborn kraut!" Freeman snapped. "You wouldn't trust your own mother!"

Heinrich said slowly, "No, I would not trust my own mother. We rest, yes?"

Freeman smacked a fist into his open hand and sat down on a rock.

The second day went slower than the first. Heinrich's strength had flagged rapidly during the morning search, and he was barely able to get out of his bunk in the afternoon.

Cleo spoke to Harry about the old man. "This is going to kill him, this pressure. Gene is always right there pushing. Yes, and so are you."

"I told you to keep out of this."

"We'll all be out of it if Max can't find this—this marker of his."

Harry went to the coaming, gripped it with both hands and stared out at the water sparkling in the sunlight.

"Why is this so important, Harry?" she asked.

He didn't answer and Cleo went below to see to Heinrich.

An hour later the old man's strength had returned to a fair degree, and once more the boat was rowed ashore. But by night-fall, the elusive marker was still to be found.

In the hours of early morning the wind backed toward the east, and what had been a calm anchorage, grew choppy. The motion of the boat woke Cleo, and though the first light of the new day had barely broken toward the east, she went into the gal-ley, put water on to boil, and stepped out on the deck.

The shape of the island emerged from the darkness to star-board. She breathed deeply of the cool morning air, feeling a deep sensuality, a vague desire, stronger than at any time since they had gotten to the islands.

Fleetingly, she thought that if Harry did not change, she just might resort to Gene Freeman. Physical need was a reality with Cleo, as it had been all her adult life. It was a thing she had grown to accept, and if wantonness became a part of it through neces-sity, then that, too, would have to be accepted.

The kettle began to whistle in the galley, and she hurried below so that it would not wake the others. She mixed her coffee, took a swallow of it, steaming hot and black. The day was com-ing very quickly. Already, through the window of the galley, she could make out the trees on the island.

Someone groaned in the forward cabin and a light came on. He began to cough. It was Heinrich. Cleo went forward to the bulkhead.

"Max? Max, are you allright?"

"*Guten Morgen,* Cleo." The old man was sitting up on the edge of the bunk, his handkerchief to his mouth.

Across from him, on the other bunk, Freeman's eyes were open. "You sick, Max?"

The German shrugged slightly and turned to Cleo. "Would you be so kind as to get me a little brandy, *Liebchen?* Perhaps this much?" He lifted his hand and held his thumb and forefinger apart.

"Do you think—"

"Get the stuff for him, Cleo," Freeman said. "This is a poor time for a temperance lecture."

Cleo shot him a scathing look, then spoke again to Heinrich. "How about a cup of coffee first? I'll fix you some eggs, if you like. We still have half a dozen."

Heinrich smiled at her. "You try to do what you believe is best for me. For that I am grateful. But please, the brandy? Perhaps then we will have the other." He began to cough again, racking, steady, as if he would never stop. His thin body shook and his face, usually wan and pale, grew red.

Harry came in from the main cabin. "Is he sick? Is something wrong with Max?"

"Would you care?" Cleo said.

He gave her a puzzled look, then brushed by into the forward cabin. "What's the matter with him, Gene?"

"I heard him all night, coughing, moaning. Maybe we ought to take a run back into town and let a doctor have a look at him."

"I will be allright," Heinrich said. "As soon as I have my brandy I will be better."

Cleo returned with a glass and the bottle. She poured an ounce or so and handed it to the old man. He nodded his thanks and drank it down.

Freeman and Harry watched him intently, waiting to see if he really did improve. Heinrich swallowed, closed his eyes and lowered the glass. After several seconds he opened his eyes. The pitch of the boat as it pulled against the anchor had grown more pronounced even since Cleo had gotten up. Heinrich put one hand down on the bunk to steady himself.

"Well?" said Freeman, expectantly.

"I—I don't know ..."

"Look," Freeman said, stepping close to the old man and taking hold of his shoulders. "Look, Heinrich. I don't give a goddamn how you feel, do you understand? We ain't out here for your health! Now get your ass out of that sack and let's get busy! "

"Leave him alone," Cleo said, pushing between the two men. Freeman hadn't expected this move from her and he was shoved back against his own bunk.

"*Nein*. Gene is right," the old man said, easing himself off the edge of the bunk. "We are not here for my health. Let us eat and then we go ashore." He smiled weakly at Cleo. "Perhaps this is the day I will find it."

"Get breakfast ready, Cleo," Harry said brusquely.

For a moment longer she regarded the German, then turned and went to the galley. She broke the last of the fresh eggs into a bowl and put bacon in the frying pan. Harry paused beside her and mixed himself a cup of instant coffee.

"If I were you," Cleo said, "I think I would be a little easier on Max."

"You keep out of it."

"I know you don't give a damn about Max himself, but have you stopped to think that he's your only key? If you kill him, you and your old chum Gene are out in the cold."

Harry took a swallow of the coffee, his eyes straight ahead. "We're not going to kill him. We'll take it easier today."

Cleo looked at her husband. It couldn't be the money that was making him the way he was—determined, almost desperate. What was it?

Freeman came in from the forward cabin. "Harry, Max—he's not kidding. I think he's sick. He passed out just a second ago.

Out cold. I—I think we better get him back to town and let a doctor take a look at him."

Cleo put the fork down quickly and started forward. Harry took hold of her arm.

"Let her go to him," Freeman said. "Maybe she can help. My God, Harry, if anything happens to Heinrich—"

Harry's grip loosened on her arm. "Go ahead." He rubbed a hand across his chin. "See what you can do for him."

"I'm not a nurse, Harry. I'll do what I can but I think Gene is right. Let's get him back to a doctor."

The *Belle* arrived in St. Ursula in midmorning, and Harry Gregory pulled to shore at the quay just below Marla Keever's office.

Heinrich's condition had improved only slightly during the four-hour run from the east end of the islands. He had regained consciousness shortly after the boat got under way, and Cleo had tucked him back in his bunk and tended him as best she could.

When the boat had been tied up, Harry told Freeman to go find the taxi. "I'll run over to Vansant's place and pick up the car later. This way we'll save time getting Max checked by a doctor."

"Harry," Freeman said. "I think we'd better make Max talk. If he conks out without telling us how he's got that dough marked, that's all she wrote."

"We'll talk about that later. Go over to Marla's office. Maybe she can find that guy with the cab."

Freeman went ashore and trotted across the quay to the office.

"Why you doing this, Harry?" Cleo wanted to know.

Gregory looked at her strangely. There seemed to be anger in his eyes as he turned away. "There's a lot of money involved. I never heard you say you didn't like money, Cleo."

Beyond Harry she saw someone coming across the quay. It was Casey Stribling. He stopped at the side of the boat. "Anything wrong?" he asked. "I thought you folks were going to be out a week or two."

"The old man's not feeling well," Harrry said, obviously not happy at the intrusion.

"Anything I can do?"

"You can mind your own goddamn business!" Harry shot back. He turned on his heel and went below.

"Please don't pay any attention to him," Cleo said. "Maybe you can help. I suppose there's a doctor on the island?"

Stribling nodded. "Two doctors. Walter Heath and Doc Miller. I heard Miller had an accident though, so you'd better contact Heath. He's in the phone directory."

Freeman came out of the office across the cobbled street, and at the same instant the cab rounded the corner and pulled up on the quay. Cleo felt strangely that she had been cheated out of spending any more time talking to Casey Stribling.

CHAPTER SIX

D R. WALTER HEATH was a short, fat man with a shining bald head. He arrived at the house in an old Lincoln with a torn and patched canvas top. The top was down, though it was obvious from the manner in which the medical man was perspiring that the noon sun was causing him great discomfort. Cleo, who had been waiting on the front porch for him, introduced herself and ushered him into the house.

"Ah, yes, Mrs. Gregory," the doctor said, looking curiously about him as he entered. "I heard there were some Americans leasing the Carleton place and I've been hoping to meet you." He glanced quickly at Cleo. "Heard there was a German fellow staying up here, too."

"It's Mr. Heinrich we've called you about, Dr. Heath. He's right in here." She showed him into the bedroom.

Heinrich was propped up in the bed, a glass in his hands.

"This is Dr. Heath," Cleo said to him.

Heath nodded pleasantly and put his black bag down on the table beside the bed. Harry and Freeman came in and Cleo introduced them to the doctor.

"If you don't mind, Mrs. Gregory," Heath said, taking her elbow and steering her toward the door. "And you gentlemen, please. I'd prefer to examine the patient alone."

The doctor closed the bedroom door behind the three of them. Freeman started to open the door to go back in, but Harry stopped him.

"I don't like that guy's looks," Freeman said glumly. Harry turned at the door and called for Irene. When she came he told her to prepare lunch.

"You knew he was sick, Gene," Harry said. "What's he got?"

Freeman shrugged his shoulders. "How should I know? If you spent the last fifteen or sixteen years in a Russian prison, how the hell do you think you'd feel?"

"If we could get him to tell us how he marked the place," Harry said, half to himself.

Freeman laughed and shook his head. "For some strange reason, Harry, he doesn't trust us."

"You talk to him, Cleo," Harry said with sudden inspiration. "He likes you. He trusts you—"

Cleo shook her head firmly. "Leave me out of it."

"It might work," Freeman said, pulling at the tip of his nose. "It just might work."

Cleo went to the edge of the patio and looked out at the sea. "What you want is a Trojan horse." She turned and glared at the two men. "Well, find one somewhere else."

Harry went toward her, his jaw firm. "I'm not asking you. I'm *telling* you."

Irene came out of the house with a tray of sandwiches and placed them on the table.

"Irene," Freeman said. "What do you know about this doctor?"

"Dr. Heath, sah?" She shook her head and turned to go. "I do not know anything."

Freeman got up and caught her arm. "Come on now. You people here know everything about everybody. Where'd he come from?"

"He came here from the United States," she said hesitantly. She tried to pull away from Freeman but he kept his grip.

"How long ago? Why did he come here?"

The woman looked around, her eyes appealing to Cleo for help. Freeman tightened his grip.

"You like your job here, Irene? Jobs like this don't come along every day. We can get somebody else."

She glanced quickly toward the open door, then said, "Dr. Heath bad doctor before he come to islands."

"Bad doctor?" said Harry, frowning.

"Yes, sah. He take babies, get into trouble, run away."

"Take babies?"

Freeman withdrew his hand threw his head back, laughing. "The old boy was an abortionist! "

Inside the house a door closed. Dr. Heath came out, his round face puckered in a frown. His eyes settled on Harry. "He's not well, Mr. Gregory."

"I gathered that much, Heath," Harry said sarcastically. "How long before he'll be able to get around?"

"And just what's his trouble?" Freeman put in.

"It's difficult to say," the doctor answered, rubbing his hands together slowly. "I'd like to get him down to the public health clinic in the village as soon as I can, perhaps in a day or two. We have an X-ray there and—"

"A *day* or two!" Freeman exploded. "Look! I want the old man out of that bed tomorrow morning!"

The doctor smiled unctuously and held out a hand. "Mr. Freeman, I am giving you my opinion as a medical man. If you do not care to listen, then you are certainly free to inquire elsewhere."

Freeman snorted and turned away.

"Very adroit, Heath," Harry said with a smile. "You know the only other doctor on the island is out of action. Calm down, Gene, and let's see what the good doctor has to say."

"Thank you, sir." Heath made a little bow toward Harry. "I'd say that Mr. Heinrich is suffering from a form of exhaustion. Physically, he appears to be extremely weak. I would definitely prescribe a prolonged rest and, of course, further examination. Yes, he will definitely need watching."

"Is there anything you can give him?" Freeman inquired. "Something that would put a little life into him for, say, a couple of weeks?"

Heath laughed uneasily. "I'm afraid a thing of that nature would be against my, ah, better judgment. The man needs building up, not tearing down."

"In other words, it wouldn't be ethical?" Freeman went on, his eyes narrowing.

The doctor nodded. "It could be interpreted that way."

"Is that so. Well—"

Harry put his hand on Freeman's arm and interrupted. "That's enough for now, Gene."

"I want this quack to *do* something!"

"Now see here!" Heath spluttered, his round face growing purple, his jowls shaking. "Mr. Gregory, sir! I do not have to take insults—"

Harry smiled affably. "How about a drink, Dr. Heath? I'm afraid Mr. Freeman lost his temper for a moment. Irene!" He looked around for the servant, who was nowhere to be seen. "Cleo, get us something to drink. Gin and tonic, Dr. Heath?"

"That would be fine, sir," the doctor managed, his feathers still ruffled.

Three-quarters of an hour later, with two gins under his belt and his feelings somewhat assuaged, the doctor got into his battered automobile and drove away.

When the car had disappeared, Freeman said to Harry, "The old buzzard thinks he's onto something. Mark my word, he's going to try to worm into this thing. He's as crooked as a snake."

"It takes one to know one," Cleo observed drily. "Harry, I think I'll go down to the village and do some shopping."

Harry, a preoccupied look on his face, nodded. "Yeah. That's a good idea. Call Mobley and have him drive you down. We may need the car."

The cab arrived and Tiger Mobley, grinning with pleasure, helped Cleo into the rear seat and drove down the hill toward the village. As she rode, Cleo wondered about the doctor. She found herself inclined to agree, however reluctantly, with the observations of Freeman.

They reached the village and Cleo leaned forward to tap the ex-boxer on the shoulder. "You can let me out anywhere, Tiger. I'm just going to do a little shopping."

He nodded and pulled over to the curb. Cleo took a bill from her purse but he shook his battered head firmly. "I—I ain't gonna charge you nothin', Miss Cleo."

"You've got to, Tiger. You're in business—"

The head-shaking persisted. "No—I like to drive you around."

"Well . . . " She smiled and dropped the bill on the seat beside him. "You keep this for me. If I ever need it I'll ask you for it."

She walked into the shop. When she came out ten minutes later, the cab still stood at the curb.

"Tiger," she said patiently, "I won't *need* you. Go find yourself a fare."

But when she came out of a second shop, he had pulled up before the door and was grinning at her.

It was like trying to shoo away a persistent fly. "Tiger, please! There's no need for you to follow me about this way. I'm going to spend the afternoon in the village and I won't need you." Suddenly, Cleo felt as if she had reprimanded a child too harshly. A hurt look came to the scarred face.

"I—I ain't got nothing else to do. You might want to—want to go someplace," he said.

Cleo smiled and touched his arm. She nodded. "Allright. Do whatever you want."

She strolled along the bright sunlit street, wandering into shops, smiling and speaking to those who spoke to her.

"You'd better watch out. They lie in wait for tourists around here."

She turned at the sound of the voice and found herself looking into the deeply tanned, smiling face of Casey Stribling.

"Oh? Then perhaps I need a guide."

A coil of new rope was slung over his shoulder. He walked to the edge of the street and tossed the rope into the front seat of an old car. "Maybe you do at that. Now, as a qualified guide, I'm going up to the hotel. Would you care to come along?"

Cleo felt a sudden lift. She started to accept, then thought better of it. "No, thank you. I'm sure you're busy," she said.

"I'm going up there on business. I've got a one-day charter set for tomorrow with some people who're staying at the hotel. I have to pick up a check from them. But that'll only take a couple of minutes. Come on." He came to her and took her arm. The contact sent a shiver through Cleo.

"I—allright. If you're sure I won't be in the way."

Stribling laughed. "Get in."

As she leaned to get into the car, she glimpsed Tiger Mobley sitting in his cab behind them. He was looking at her, his brow Wrinkled in a frown.

Stribling drove the car up the winding roadway to the north of town. The hotel stood on the summit of the highest hill, overlooking the town and the harbor to the south and the dark green hills that rolled toward the shore of the island to the north. Cleo waited in the hotel bar while Stribling attended to his business.

She had hardly had time to taste her gin and tonic before he joined her. He slid onto the stool beside her.

"Hello, Cap'n Casey," the Negro bartender said. He placed a jigger of whiskey on the bar, a glass of water next to it, and ambled away to wait on his other customers.

"You're no stranger here," Cleo said, smiling.

"In my business it pays to have these people on my side."

"Have you lived here all your life?"

Stribling tossed his whiskey off and sipped the water. He shook his head. "I've been here for about fifteen years. I'm from Indiana."

"Would I be prying if I were to ask how you came to be here? Not everyone from Indiana runs a schooner in the Caribbean."

"No mystery, I'm afraid. After the war I had a job with a shipping company in New York. They had an office here and I was sent down to operate it. I fell in love with the islands when I first set eyes on them, and when the time came about a year later for me to transfer back to the States, I quit. I took a job here at the hotel for a month or two, right here behind this bar. Then I worked for Vansant down at the boatyard. That's where I happened onto the *Antares*."

"The what?"

He reached into his shirt pocket and took out a card. Cleo read it. *Schooner Antares for charter. Day, week, month. Contact Captain Stribling.*

She handed the card back to him. "It doesn't say how to contact Captain Stribling."

He slipped the card back into his pocket. "You forget you're not back in New York, Cleo. Down here all you have to do is ask the first person you run into, and he can tell you anything you want to know about anyone else on the island."

He motioned for the bartender to pour him another drink, after seeing that Cleo's glass was still half full. "Now take you people, for example."

"Us?" she said, looking at him in surprise.

"Very mysterious. Everybody's making all sorts of guesses."

Cleo laughed, thinking of Harry's secretive ways, his efforts to be inconspicuous, and the results they had had. Stribling looked at her inquiringly and she said, "Just a private joke."

He nodded. "How do you like the islands?"

Cleo looked down into her glass, her face growing thoughtful. "That's an odd thing. I didn't want to come down here at all. But something happens. It gets to you—sort of grows on you."

"Island fever," Stribling said. "Some people get it, some don't. You've got it."

She laughed and took a swallow of her drink. "Yes, I suppose I have."

A woman came in from the hotel lobby, caught Cleo's eye and started toward them.

"Here comes Marla Keever," Cleo said.

Stribling did not seem to be particularly pleased by the news. He glanced around, then turned back to his drink.

"Well, hello there!" Marla said. She took the bar stool on the other side of Stribling, looked at him for a moment, then at Cleo. "What brings you two up here?"

"I'm here about a charter," he said. "Mrs. Gregory came along for the ride."

Marla's eyebrows rose exaggeratedly and she motioned to the bartender. He placed a drink before her. It seemed to Cleo that he knew exactly what everybody in St. Ursula drank.

"I heard your guest was ill, Cleo," she said. "Nothing serious, I hope."

"Dr. Heath is attending to him." News did travel fast.

"Ugh! Too bad you couldn't get Miller. Walter is a grimy little bastard. Do anything for a buck." She took a deep swallow of her drink. "He was an abortionist back in the States, you know. Still would be if there was any need for one down here. Trouble is, all us imports are up on the latest in contraceptives, and the natives don't give a damn if they have a hundred kids."

Stribling finished his drink and stood up. He said to Cleo, "Ready to go? I've got to get back to the boat."

"Uh-huh." She got up and nodded to Marla.

"I hope I didn't run you off," Marla said. The woman's candor was a little more than was called for, Cleo thought, particularly with a stranger.

"As Casey said, I only came along for the ride."

Marla's smile was not without meaning. "Sure," she said. "Just for the ride." She put her hand on Stribling's arm as he picked up his change from the bar. "Drop around later, huh? I haven't seen much of you lately."

"I've got a charter for tomorrow," he said, avoiding her eyes. "I'll try to make it, but chances are I'll be busy. Eddie's been on a binge the past few days and I've got to see about everything."

"I'll give you a hand," Marla said quickly.

He started to say something, shrugged, and took Cleo's arm. In the car, Cleo asked, "Who's Eddie?"

"A kid who helps out sometimes on the *Antares*." He offered no further conversation on the ride back to the village.

The following morning Dr. Heath came to the house at ten and went in to see Heinrich. He was closeted with the German for nearly an hour.

Gene Freeman paced up and down the patio like an expectant father. "This guy is up to something, Harry! I don't like the way he's putting us off about Max. He's trying to find out what we're doing down here. The sonofabitch suspects something's up and he wants to count himself in! "

Cleo thought of what Casey had said the day before about the curiosity of the islanders about them. She laid aside the book she had been trying to read. "Did it ever occur to you that Max is simply too sick to go tramping around the islands?"

"Why don't you go down to the beach and take yourself a swim," Harry suggested pointedly. "Gene and I can handle what has to be done here."

She had felt restless all morning. In an hour she had hardly read a dozen pages of the book. She found herself recalling the hours spent yesterday with Casey, found herself wondering about his approach to life, and then envying it and, finally, to a degree, accepting it.

She felt a hand on her shoulder. It was Freeman. His fingers moved to her neck and began a slow, massaging motion. She looked around quickly and saw that Harry had gone into the house.

"Cleo, you know you're driving me just a little crazy, don't you?" Freeman said. "I'll give it to you straight. I've never wanted any woman the way I want you. I'm not a bad guy when you get to know me. Now Harry, he's no good for you. Just try me, baby—"

She jerked away and stood up, her eyes blazing at him. "I'm far from being a prude, Gene. But you turn my stomach! I can't put it any plainer than that."

She went to the edge of the patio and stared down at the ocean, her breasts rising and falling rapidly with her quickened breathing. Maybe a swim would help calm her. She turned, picked up a towel, and went to the head of the steps leading down to the beach.

"Tell Harry I took his advice and went for a swim," she said to Freeman. "And you take my advice, Gene. You leave me alone, do you understand me? You keep your filthy hands off me!"

Freeman laughed briefly. "I must be getting to you, Cleo. You wouldn't be that sore over a couple of passes unless you were weakening."

"You conceited—" Without finishing her sentence, she whirled and started down the steep stairs.

Her anger had ameliorated by the time she got to the beach. She hung the towel over the end of the banister and walked to the edge of the water. There she paused, turning and looking back up toward the house. Freeman was standing at the patio wall. He waved his hand and his teeth glistened in the sunlight. She knew he would stay there, watching her. She looked to her right. The beach curved close in to the dense growth of the hillside.

A hundred yards down the beach she would he out of sight of anyone on the patio above. She picked up her towel and soon found herself on a secluded section of beach, bounded on one side by the broad, empty expanse of the sea, and on the other by the hillside. The place had the feeling of a sanctuary—a place for solitude or, perhaps, for love-making. Her thoughts went unbidden to Casey Stribling and she smiled, wondering what he would do if he knew the uninhibited ideas she had involving him.

Cleo went to the edge of the beach and spread the towel on the sand.

She looked back toward the place where the beach curved. She did not think Freeman would follow her down. He would want to talk to Dr. Heath and Harry. At the moment, Heinrich's cache meant more to him than anything else.

The beach was isolated and completely deserted. There were no houses on the side of the hill the nearest one was at least a mile to the south. She unsnapped the halter of her bikini and dropped it onto the towel. Then she removed the lower part of the suit.

Naked and unfettered, she ran across the beach to the water and dove into a wave. She swam straight out, feeling the soothing coolness of the water enveloping her body.

After a time she stopped and looked back at the shore. For a moment she was surprised by the distance she had covered, but she had always been an excellent swimmer, and knew how to conserve her strength. She rested for a while and then she began to swim back, more slowly than she had come out.

When she stopped again, her feet settled to the sand. She stood in the shallows, letting the breakers crest around her, cascading water over her back and shoulders and in her short-clipped red hair. There was something about a beach, the sea and a deserted shore that aroused Cleo. There was a primitive feel to it, and again she found her thoughts centered very definitely on Casey Stribling.

She walked up the shelving beach, clear of the water, and stopped, letting the water drip from her body. The sun was hot and the breeze that cut across the water where she had been swimming was broken by the hills behind the beach.

She walked to the towel and took a cigarette from the pack she had dropped there. She stood, legs spread apart, and suddenly she sensed that she was not alone. She looked around quickly. Had Freeman followed her, after all? Was he standing there in the shadows, behind the trunk of a palm, waiting?

Cleo dropped the cigarette and reached down quickly for the bathing suit. There was a rustling in the jungle-like growth ten yards from where she stood.

"Who—who is it?" she called out.

She saw movement again in the deep shadows and then he stepped out into the sunlight.

"Tiger!" Cleo exclaimed. A sudden feeling of relief swept over her. "You followed me here, Tiger?"

The big man nodded, smiling. His eyes went quickly over her and he moved closer. "I—I been watching you. I been there in the woods."

"That wasn't very nice of you," Cleo said. "Now you turn around while I put this suit on."

The big man said nothing. It was as if he hadn't heard her at all. He stood with his huge hands hanging at his sides, his chin thrust slightly forward, his beady eyes riveted to Cleo's nude body.

"Tiger ... " she said, not at all sure of herself now. She had been thinking of him as a simple child, a harmless creature who had been rendered incapable of emotion.

She bent and picked up the towel quickly, holding it before her. He shook his head and moved toward her again, his canvas shoes soundless on the sand.

"No!" Cleo exclaimed, backing away, her attention focused on him with the fascination of a rabbit watching the approach of a hungry snake. Her heel caught over an exposed root at the edge of the beach. She fell backwards, the towel only partially covering her. Mobley made a grunting sound and hovered over her.

Real fear caught at her. She tried to scramble again to her feet, but Mobley put out one powerful hand and took hold of her arm.

"I—I ain't gonna hurt you," he muttered.

"You just go away and leave me alone! Go on! Do as I say, Tiger, or you'll get yourself into trouble!"

He kept his eyes on her, completely heedless of what she had said. With a sudden twist, Cleo pulled free of him. Dropping the covering towel, she whirled and ran along the beach as fast as her legs would carry her. There was no time to look back. Flight was her only defense now; she knew that by the strange look on Tiger Mobley's battered face. He was a study in single-mindedness.

Behind her she heard him breathing and mumbling something as he ran in pursuit. Then her legs were caught in a tight grip and she was flung forward by her own momentum onto the warm, dry sand.

His arms were about her ankles where he had tackled her, rendering her legs immobile. She pulled at the sand with her hands but, even as she tried again to break free, she felt his hand grip the back of one thigh and his weight moving up her bare legs. His open hand spread over her buttocks and slid to her waist, his fingers hard and rough.

"I wouldn't—hurt you—" he said. "Don't try to run off again. I ain't gonna—gonna hurt you."

Cleo opened her mouth and screamed as loud as she could. There would be no one to hear her, she knew that, but it was all she could do under the circumstances.

"Please—Miss Cleo—don't you do that."

"Tiger, you can't do this! You mustn't do this! No—"

Both his hands gripped her waist and, as if she were a doll, he rose, lifting her from the sand. When she was on her feet he pulled her back against him, his grip firm yet tender. One arm went about her waist while his free hand came up and the fingertips brushed across her breasts.

Cleo swung back with her right elbow, stabbing into his ribs. She kicked back at his shins, but neither action seemed to have the slightest effect on him. It seemed that the harder she struggled against the massive power holding her, the more secure became his grip on her.

"Somebody might come along the beach," she gasped. "You'll—you'll get caught—you'll be in trouble—" Still she swung back with her elbow, digging hard at him.

His hand moved gently over her breasts, the tips of his fingers tracing over the hard nipples.

Suddenly he picked her up, turning her in his arms as if she were a baby, and walked quickly up the beach. Cleo looked up into his face. It was easy to see that reasoning would not get her out of the situation in which she found herself.

The face was not that of a rational man, or even that of a man engulfed in passion, unable to back down from the stand he had taken. It was the face of an animal, neither benign nor malevolent. The lumpy, battered features were frozen with purpose.

She writhed in his arms, trying to break the grip. Tiger came to an outcropping of huge rocks and carried Cleo into a grotto, where he knelt on the sand and put her down on her back, holding her with one hand pressed against her belly.

"Tiger—please—"

His eyes told her that talk would get her nowhere. Suddenly she found her struggles weakening. There was something about him, the forceful yet tender way he caressed her.

"No—Tiger—"

The hands that had been tearing at him relaxed, and Cleo felt the old longing, the need, welling up within her.

My God, she thought frantically, *what's happening to me? I'm being raped and I like it.*

Her hands moved across his broad, hard back and she offered herself to him. The reluctant part of her was quiescent, even pleading.

"Yes! *yes!*"

The moist sand beneath the overhanging rocks was cool against her back. He came to her now not like an attacker, but like a lover, as if this were some prearranged and longed for tryst.

Gone was the clumsy and almost pitiful creature she had come to see him as, and in its place was a skillful, considtrate lover. His hands were like a balm as they moved over her. Everything left her mind. Her brain became alive with pure sensation, with the here and now. The sun and sea faded away. Her entire being rose to heights she had not attained in many years.

"*Now ... oh, yes ...* " Her breath came in gasps and her arms tightened about the powerful body, trying to pull him even closer as she floated in a fiery cloud, completely detached from everything, living in this single reality.

She did not know for some time that he had at last pulled away from her and had moved off soundlessly to disappear into the trees and underbrush on the hillside.

CHAPTER SEVEN

FOR A LONG WHILE she was only vaguely aware of the sound of water breaking on a shore. The first conscious thought was of something Marla Keever had said about Tiger, about his being handy at a lot of things. Now she knew what Marla had meant.

She raised herself on one elbow and looked about. There was no sign of him. He had vanished into the thicket and was probably up there somewhere on the hillside, scrambling along like a big animal. He *was* an animal. There had been nothing malevolent in what he had done. He had heeded his desires completely, and without complication.

Slowly Cleo got to her feet, brushing the sand from her body. She walked to the water and waded out. Her feeling was not that of an violated woman; rather it was one of release, of almost perverse satisfaction at what had happened to her, as if this in some far-out sense was a sort of vengeance on Harry for his coolness, his perverse teasing.

I've just been raped and I'm smiling, she said to herself.

She came out of the surf and put on the scanty bathing suit. Her eyes wandered over the dense green of the hillside, and she wondered if he was still up there someplace, perhaps thinking about coming down again.

Cleo grinned and slung the towel over her shoulder. Island fever, that was what she had. And she hadn't been raped at all. It had begun as that, but somewhere along the line acquiescence sneaked in, and then outright enthusiasm.

She walked around the long bend of the beach and climbed the steps to the house, dropping the towel over the stone border of the patio.

Freeman sat quietly in a rattan chair, looking at her over the rim of a glass. "Have a good swim?"

"Very good, thank you."

"I'd have joined you but Harry and I had to talk to Heath."

Cleo fluffed her damp hair and went to the table where the gin and tonic stood on a tray. She mixed herself a drink. "Is there any news on Max?"

"I don't know. Heath's still in there with him."

"Here he comes now," Cleo said, looking past Freeman to the door.

Harry and the doctor came out, the medical man rubbing his double chin thoughtfully. "I don't know, Mr. Gregory. If you could tell me something about Mr. Heinrich's past—"

"That's none of your business, Heath," Freeman put in bluntly. "You know all you need to know. Just tell us what to do."

Heath, for the first time, faced up to Freeman on his own terms. "I know there's one thing you're extremely afraid of, and that is the possibility that Heinrich may die."

"Is he—is he *that* bad?"

"He could be," the doctor said gravely. "I gather that Heinrich is not here in the islands for his health; that there is some other reason for his being here." He paused beside the liquor tray and glanced inquiringly at Harry.

"Help yourself," Harry said.

"Thank you." Heath prepared himself a drink. "As I was saying, Mr. Heinrich seems to be a very ill man. Nothing short of an extended rest will do him the slightest good."

"To hell with doing him *good*," Freeman snapped. "What can we do to get him back on that boat?"

"I was coming to that." Heath swirled his drink slowly. He gazed down thoughtfully into the glass. "It might come to something more than my, ah, regular fee. In addition, he would need a professional attendant."

"How about coming along yourself?" Harry said.

Heath shook his head. "I'm afraid I can't at the moment. I have several patients I can't leave. However," he went on, looking up, "we could ask Marla Keever if she would go along."

"Marla?"

He nodded. "Marla is—or was—a nurse. She'd do very nicely on a case such as this."

Freeman headed for the house. "I'll call her." At the door he paused. "If she'll come along, when can we go out again?"

The doctor took a swallow of his drink and pursed his lips. "At once, Mr. Freeman. That would suit you, wouldn't it?"

Marla had accepted the proposition with alacrity, and now she sat on the patio and took the glass Harry held out to her. She had just gotten instructions from Heath as to the care of the patient, and the doctor had gone, seemingly with some reluctance.

"I've been looking for an excuse to get away for a while," Marla said with a smile. "Besides, I love a mystery."

"What's the mystery?" Harry said.

"Oh, come off it! You people are the biggest mystery that's hit St. Ursula in years!"

"Just vacationers, that's all."

She laughed. "What's all this walking the old man has to do? If he was on vacation, he'd be flat on his back. Heath told me that much."

"Heath?" said Freeman, suspicion edging his voice. "Did he say anything else?"

Marla sipped her drink. "You're worried about Walter? Well, don't. Oh, he knows something funny is going on. I think he smells money, and he wants to get his grubby little hands on it. But he's nothing to worry about."

"Can you be ready to leave tomorrow morning?" Harry asked.

"I'm ready any time."

Harry nodded. "Good." He turned toward Freeman. "I'll drive over to the boatyard before dawn and get the boat. You bring Max and Cleo and I'll meet all of you at the quay across from Marla's office. That way we don't have to get Max up so early."

"Okay," Freeman agreed, nodding.

"We'll spend the rest of this afternoon rounding up supplies and whatever else we might need," Harry said. "Marla, have you got the medication Max will need?"

"I've got the prescriptions. I'll pick it up at the apothecary in the village." She took a long swallow of her drink and crossed her legs. "Are you going to let me die of curiosity?"

"What?"

"What cooks? We're hunting for something, is that it?" She looked from Harry to Freeman to Cleo. "Walter Heath smells dough. Is he right? Is this some kind of a treasure hunt?"

The day had exhausted Cleo emotionally as well as physically. She had gone to bed early and had fallen into untroubled sleep. Now, deep in her sleep, she heard the ringing of a bell. A telephone was ringing, pulling her up toward consciousness.

She opened her eyes just as the lamp on the night table snapped on and Harry, propped up on one elbow, puffy-eyed, jerked the phone off its cradle.

"Hello? Who the hell is this? It's three o'clock in the morning!" The bedcovers rustled as he sat up, swinging his feet to the floor and reaching almost automatically for the pack of cigarettes on the table. "Vansant? What's the—? *What?*"

Cleo sat up in her bed and looked at him. Harry's eyes were wide, his mouth open. The unlighted cigarette dropped from his fingers.

"You must be imagining things," he said. "Wait a minute! I can see the harbor from the front of the house. You hang on!"

"What happened?" Cleo inquired. He ignored her, jumping to his feet and running from the room.

"What's all the fuss?" Freeman demanded, snagging him on the way out. "I heard the phone."

"It's Vansant at the boatyard. The boat's burning!"

Cleo pushed her arms into her robe and ran through the living room. The two men were already outside on the front lawn, staring down toward the harbor. Cleo stopped beside Harry. The moon was behind a bank of clouds, and the blaze on the distant side of the harbor was unmistakable. As they stood watching, something exploded, throwing a burst of orange flame skyward.

"That must have been the gas tank."

"Did he—did he say what happened?" Freeman asked.

"He's still on the phone." Harry stood watching the distant flames as if hypnotized by the spectacle.

"I'd better talk to him." Freeman turned and went quickly back into the house.

Somewhere behind them a night bird called lonesomely. The breeze had died during the flight and a heavy, almost oppressive silence seemed to hang over them as they watched the fire far across the harbor.

"Well, that does it," Harry said, his voice so low Cleo hardly understood him.

"Was he sure it was the *Belle?*"

Harry nodded. "He was sure."

Freeman rejoined them. "There wasn't anything to be done as far as Vansant was concerned. That ancient rattletrap they call a fire truck is there now, but they can't reach the boat."

"I know. I anchored it out."

"Well..." Freeman said, one hand moving nervously about his face. "A bad break. Nothing we can do standing out here. I could use a drink and I suppose you could, too—both of you."

He went back into the house. Harry turned after a few seconds and followed him. He stopped at the door and waited for Cleo to join him. Without looking at her he said, "I think we had better have that drink."

Freeman stood at the bar in his pajamas. He lit a cigarette, inhaled deeply, and arranged three glasses before him. "It'll just be a delay." He dropped ice cubes into the glasses and, seeing Max come into the room, took a fourth glass off the shelf.

"What is happening?" the German asked.

Harry told him about the boat burning. Freeman passed the drinks around and sat down, tinkling the ice in his drink. "We'll have to get another boat. Probably be able to locate one in San Juan—"

"With what?" Harry said flatly.

"With what—?" Freeman's eyes widened and a puzzled expression crossed his face. "I thought you'd have the answer, not the question, Harry."

"I never thought about insuring the boat." Harry scratched his cheek and cast a sidelong glance at Cleo. "The three of you better take a good long swallow of that booze. There's no more money." He slapped his free hand against his chest in a slow rhythm. "Harry Gregory is broke. Flat. Stony! "

Heinrich was the only one who did not stare at him. It was Freeman who spoke first. "This is a hell of a time for a joke, Harry. We've got to make *plans*. The best bet is to charter a plane to get you back to San Juan. You can—"

"It's no joke," Harry said flatly. He got up stiffly and went across the room to the open patio door and looked out into the darkness. "I hocked my ass to get the thing this far. I doubt if I could borrow the price of a cup of coffee."

"You're—you're *serious?*" Freeman's voice cracked.

"Harry," Cleo said. She moved across the room to his side, looked into his face. "This is true? What about the company?

What about the Gregory Stores? I didn't have the slightest idea they were in trouble."

He shook his head. "Oh, *they're* not in trouble. I've been selling off my stock for years. It's all gone, every last share. You know all those business trips of mine?" He looked over at his wife, a thin smile touching his lips. "Most of 'em were trips to Vegas. I've been in trouble for quite a while, Cleo, but most people were just like you and Gene; they couldn't believe Harry Gregory was actually in financial hot water, so my credit's been good. I've got the Midas touch—in reverse."

"Come on now, Harry," Freeman said in a brittle voice. "You can get up enough for a lousy *boat!*"

"I've got enough for your ticket back to the States," Harry said to Cleo. "There's nothing to hold you here now. I'll admit it was a dirty trick to let you think there was money when it was all gone, but I'm rather fond of dirty tricks. You can pack your things whenever you're ready."

Cleo turned away, her feelings confused. She should have felt angry and vindictive toward Harry but she didn't. There was no virtue in poverty, she had long been aware of that, but neither was there virtue in money, not in using it as she had all these years. Harry's confession was going to force her to break a habit of long standing.

"We'll talk about my plans later," she said in a low voice.

Heinrich chuckled. "So your rich friend is not so rich after all, eh, Gene?"

"Shut up!"

Harry walked back to the bar and poured whiskey over the melting ice in his glass. "I don't see how that boat could just blow up. Maybe somebody's trying to stop this thing."

"If so, that someone seems to have met with success," Heinrich said.

Freeman walked over to the German. "You didn't tell Heath anything, did you, Max?"

The old man looked up at him in surprise. "Why would I tell him anything?"

"If you could cut down to one partner, you'd get half the loot instead of a third. A million's a hell of a lot more than two-thirds of a million!" Freeman reached down and roughly grabbed hold of the lapels of the old man's pajamas.

"How would I know that Harry could not buy another boat?" Heinrich said. "What good would it do me for the boat to burn?"

"He's right," Harry said. "Turn him loose."

Reluctantly Freeman loosened his grip and drew his hands back. "Maybe it was an accident."

Harry tossed off his drink. "I'm going down to Vansant's and try to find out what happened."

"What the hell for?" Freeman snapped. "What good will that do? It's all over!"

"Harry," Max said, "perhaps a boat could be chartered."

"That costs money, too."

"Yes, but perhaps someone could be induced to come in on a—a—" He groped, trying to find the word he sought.

"Contingent?" Cleo ventured.

"Yes! That is it! Such a thing is done, is it not?"

Harry tinkled the ice in his empty glass. "That's a possibility. But who around here—?"

"There is a schooner here," Max interrupted. "A fellow by the name of Stribling owns her."

Freeman shook his head vehemently. "Three's goddamn plenty in this thing! I'm against cutting in a fourth—dead set against it!"

"We must have a boat, Gene," the German said with Teutonic logic. "The search could take quite some time yet. It is possible that we have missed my marker already. We may have to begin again."

"Begin again? Why? How the devil could you have missed the damn thing?" He whirled toward Harry. "Did you hear what Heinrich said? The stupid bastard—"

"Cut it out, Gene," Harry said. "One thing at a time. In the first place, we wouldn't have to offer Stribling a full share. Maybe five percent for the use of his boat."

"He'd be crazy to come in on something like this," Cleo put in.

"Why?" Freeman stared at her. "What's so crazy about five per cent of a couple of million bucks?"

"I mean he'd be crazy to let you take his boat. He's got no reason to trust you."

"It's an idea, though," Harry said. "I'll get in touch with him in the morning. Gene, do you want to go down to Vansant's with me?"

"What? Oh, no. I'll stay here. It's a waste of time going down there."

Harry went out. The car lights flashed through briefly from the front of the house and the sound of the engine faded quickly as the car pulled away and headed down toward the harbor.

Heinrich pulled himself up from his chair. "I am going back to bed. *Gut Nacht.*"

Cleo sat with her glass in her hand, absorbed in thought. She was not aware that Freeman was still in the room till he spoke.

"How about it, Cleo? How does it feel to find out you're a sucker?"

She looked at him. "You tell me."

He shrugged. "I didn't have any reason to suspect he was broke, but you should have known."

She touched her hand to her cheek. "Yes. I suppose I should have. Looking back, it should have struck me as being out of character for Harry, letting a con man like you talk him into a treasure hunt. I can see why he fell for it now. He was desperate."

"You don't think Max is the real thing?"

"Oh, I don't know."

He came across the room and sat on the arm of her chair. "Are you going to stick with him now?"

"This isn't the time to start making plans." She glared at him. "Besides which, it's none of your damned business!"

Freeman laughed, putting his hand on her shoulder. "Want to try some of Doc Freeman's medicine? Guaranteed to make you forget your troubles."

"Oh, shut up!" She pulled away and stood up. "I'm going back to bed—alone." She put her glass down on the bar and went to the bedroom. She closed the door and started to lock it, but that meant Harry would have to wake her when he got back. Besides, she was certain that Freeman wouldn't try anything, at least not with Max and the maid both in the house.

She did not wake when Harry came back, and when she did open her eyes, the morning sun was streaming in through the open window.

The four of them were at breakfast on the patio when Casey Stribling arrived in answer to Harry's message. As he came through the house he took off his long-billed cap.

"Good morning, Stribling," Harry said, indicating a vacant chair. "Care to join us for some breakfast?"

He sat down. "I'll have some coffee, please."

"Irene, a cup for Captain Stribling."

"I heard about your boat," Casey Stribling said. "I'm sorry. How did it happen?"

Harry helped himself to the scrambled eggs and shook his head. "I went down and talked to Vansant. He said he happened to wake up and saw the fire. The boat was anchored out about thirty or forty yards. Everything was aboard and we were pulling out this morning."

"It might have been spontaneous combustion," Freeman put in. "Or maybe a short in some of the electrical equipment and gas fumes in the bilge."

The Indian woman came out of the house and placed a cup before Stribling. Cleo poured the coffee and Casey smiled his thanks.

Max put his fork down and wiped his mouth. "We have also considered the possibility that it was some sort of, ah, sabotage."

Casey's eyebrows lifted. "Is that so?"

"Well, that's over and done with," Harry said. "As I told you on the phone, Stribling, we'd like to lease your boat."

Casey glanced at him over the top of his cup. "Lease the *Antares?* I'm in the charter business, Gregory. I don't lease my boat out. I gather from your choice of words that you want the boat and not me."

Harry nodded. "We'd prefer it that way. Frankly, you've sort of got us over a barrel. We need a boat. We need one badly and you're the only possibility."

"What about insurance on your boat?" Casey looked around the patio and took a swallow of his coffee. "Everybody on the island says you people have money to burn. Why don't you fly to San Juan and buy yourself another boat?"

Harry coughed. He pushed his cup across the table. "A little more coffee please, Cleo."

"For Christ's sake, Harry," Freeman said heatedly. "Tell him the whole story and let's find out whether we can make a deal or not!"

"Allright, Gene." Harry stirred sugar into his cup. "Stribling, we do not have money to burn. The fact is, we do not even have money to pay you for your boat. But we *will* have it, a lot of it. That's why we need the boat."

Casey Stribling looked around at the four faces, his eyes stopped on Cleo. "You're down here on some kind of a—a *treasure* hunt?"

"We'll give you five per cent for the use of that tub of yours," Freeman said, leaning across the table. "What do you say? This thing could run into millions, Stribling! You could come out with a hundred grand or so just by letting us take your boat for a week or two! "

Stribling turned toward Freeman. Their eyes locked briefly, and then Casey smiled. "You're serious, aren't you? Look, have you got any idea how many people go broke every year scratching around the Caribbean looking for buried treasure? I suppose you've got the usual map—"

"We've got a hell of a lot better than any map!" Freeman said, his eyes blazing. "We've got *him!*" He poked a finger toward Max. "He's the guy who buried it!"

"He's *what?*"

"We're not telling you any more until we know where you stand," Freeman went on. "Do you want in?"

Stribling got to his feet slowly and walked across the patio. He paused at the edge and looked out at the sea. After a moment he turned and spoke to Harry. "Is this true?"

Harry nodded.

Stribling turned his eyes toward Max Heinrich. "You're a German, aren't you?"

"Yes," said Max.

"This money, it had something to do with the war?"

"Yes. I—"

Freeman jumped to his feet. "That's enough, Max. Come on, Stribling. We can't play around here all morning. Do you want in? If you do, say so!"

"Allright," he said firmly. "But you can't have just the boat. I go along, too."

"Now wait a—"

"Hold on, Gene," Harry said, holding his hand out. "It's okay. Fact is, it might even be better this way. Stribling here knows the islands." He turned toward Casey. "How about the accommodations aboard your boat? Can you take care of the five of us and yourself?"

"Five?" He looked around at the four people.

"Marla Keever's going along," Cleo said. "Max needs medical care and Heath recommended Marla."

"Marla—" He paused and rubbed his cheek thoughtfully. A thin smile touched his lips and he gave a little shrug. "Sure. The *Antares* can handle it. There's a stateroom, the main cabin, and two bunks in the forepeak."

Harry pushed back from the table and took a pack of cigarettes from his pocket. "When can you be ready to sail? We'll need supplies—"

"You haven't told me yet where we're supposed to be sailing to," Stribling said.

"The only thing we know for certain is that the cache is in this group of islands, on a north shore. We had charts aboard the *Belle* showing where we had already looked but now they're gone."

"Where were they on the boat? Maybe they didn't burn before she went down."

"It's possible, but the *Belle* sank in thirty to forty feet of water."

"I've got scuba gear aboard the *Antares*. I'll go down and take a look."

"You have what sort of gear, Captain Stribling?" Max wanted to know.

"Scuba. Self-contained underwater breathing aparatus. Aqualungs."

Max nodded. "Ah, yes." He picked up an empty glass before him, toyed with it, then smiled toward Cleo. "*Liebchen,* a bit of brandy to start the day?"

CHAPTER EIGHT

ARRY WALKED TOWARD THE DOOR with the schooner captain. "We'll see about the food and supplies while you take a look at the *Belle.* Maybe we can get away by noon."

"Allright," said Casey. "I'll meet you at the *Antares.* She's tied up at the quay."

Harry nodded. "I know where she is." He stopped, grinned at Stribling and put out his hand. "Welcome to the treasure hunt!"

Casey chuckled. "Sure. You know, if anybody ever told me I'd fall for the old treasure routine after all the time I've been down here, well. I'd have said they were crazy."

Cleo joined them. "Casey—" She looked quickly at her husband and then back at Stribling. "I'd like to go along with you if I may. I've never done any skin-diving and it fascinates me."

"Cleo," said Harry, "maybe Stribling hasn't got enough gear for the two of you."

"I've got two lungs. Sure, come along. It's a shallow dive, and there're no currents in the harbor. It'd be perfectly safe, Harry— if it's allright with you."

Harry frowned. "I thought maybe Cleo could take care of the groceries—"

"Let Gene do that," she said firmly, taking Stribling's arm. "Wait a second while I get my bathing suit." She turned and ran through the house.

A minute later she was seated beside Casey Stribling in his ancient automobile. Below them the town lay in bright morning sunlight. She could see the schooner at its mooring on the quay.

"Why did you decide to come along, Casey? You think we're a bunch of idiots, don't you?"

He smiled. "Maybe. But I'm an idiot, too. And I guess there's a bit of Jim Hawkins in the most skeptical of us."

"Who? Oh! Treasure Island!"

"The old man, Max—there's something about him that makes the thing a little credible. And the boat blowing up out there at Vansant's last night." He glanced over at Cleo. "Maybe there's a Long John Silver lurking around here some-place, too."

"You don't think it was an accident?"

He shrugged. "Maybe we can find out something when we dive."

They drove on through the village. Here and there a shop-keeper unlocked his door for the day's business. People smiled and waved to Casey as he passed.

"This is just another little town where everybody knows everybody else," Cleo said. She felt exhilarated, as if she were embarking on some entirely new phase of her life. Strangely, the revelation that Harry was broke had not had the expected effect on her. In a way, she felt oddly relieved.

"You can't explain it to anyone," Stribling said thoughtfully, "but the islands really get you. After you've been here awhile, and if you get that feeling, you never want to leave. You can't conceive of anyone actually walking through snow to a dingy office to sit behind a desk all day. You come to think you and you alone have found the secret of real living."

Cleo laughed and put her hand on his forearm. "You, sir, are a nature boy! A beachcomber!"

Their eyes met briefly and she took her hand away as if she had received an electrical shock.

He pulled to a stop across the street from Marla Keever's office. The schooner lay at the quay, sails furled, immobile in the still water.

"You wait here," he said, flinging open the door. "I'll go get the diving equipment."

She watched him as he trotted across to the schooner, his body straight, his movement easy and lithe.

"Hi, Cleo, what are you doing here?"

She looked around saw Marla coming toward her from the office.

"Good morning, Marla."

The woman stopped at the side of the car. She looked beyond toward the schooner, then at Cleo. "I was just trying to call your house but the line was tied up. I heard about the boat. Is the deal off?"

"Harry made an arrangement with Casey for his boat," Cleo said. "We'll be leaving this afternoon."

"Oh? Well, I've got all my stuff there in the office. I'll go ahead and lock up and put my things aboard." Again her eyes went toward the schooner. "Here comes Casey now. What's with all the diving gear?"

"We're going down to take a look at the *Belle.*"

"We? You and Casey?" Cleo sensed something more than mere curiosity in Marla's question.

Casey reached the car and opened the rear door, putting the diving equipment on the seat. "Hello, Marla."

"Hello, Captain Stribling," she said coolly.

"I hear you're going along."

"That's right. If I have the captain's approval."

He came around the car and climbed in behind the wheel. "Just put your stuff aboard. The boat's unlocked."

Cleo recalled Stribling's reaction back at the house when Harry told him Marla was coming along on the trip, and now she could almost feel the tension in Marla as she stood beside the car.

"Harry and the others will be down soon," Cleo said.

Casey put the car in gear and pulled away. They drove along in silence on the narrow street that bordered the harbor.

After a while, Cleo said, "Marla seemed a little cool, or was that my imagination?"

Casey shook his head. "I don't think it was your imagination."

"I'm poking my nose in where it isn't wanted?"

"Refreshing candor, and I ought to let it go at that. We've been here quite a while, Marla and I. We've found a few common interests and we've been—pretty good friends. I think she's developed a jealous streak, that's all."

Cleo clasped her hands in her lap and smiled inwardly. This should work into an interesting cruise.

Stribling parked outside the corrugated metal building that housed Vansant's shop and living quarters. Vansant, a deeply tanned little man in his early sixties, came out of the building at the sound of the car.

"Morning, folks. "He glanced into the car. "Going down to have a look at the remains, Casey?"

"Yeah." Casey began to unload the diving gear. "You got any ideas on what happened?"

The man shook his head. "Nope." He pointed down to the edge of the water. "You can take that skiff there. That's all that's left of Gregory's stuff—the skiff."

"Cleo," Casey said, "you can change inside. I'll slip my trunks on here in the car and wait for you at the skiff."

Cleo smiled and went inside the building. As she removed her clothes and picked up the bikini, she thought of Tiger Mobley and of what had taken place on the beach yesterday. She let one hand brush down over the lush curves of her body and found herself thinking some very intimate thoughts concerning Casey Stribling.

With a little laugh, she donned the suit and went out. Stribling had already changed and was standing at the harbor's edge talking to Vansant.

It was Vansant who saw her first, the look of pure pleasure on his weathered face causing Casey to turn. Both men grinned their appreciation. Cleo ran a hand through her red hair and smiled back, swaying her body exaggeratedly as she came to join them.

Casey helped her on with the air tank and the breathing device, instructing her in its use. "Just stick close to me and you'll be okay." He turned to the yard owner. "Approximately where did she sink?"

"About thirty or forty yards, right out there," the older man said, pointing. "The explosion must have cracked the hull, because she went down pretty quick."

Casey looked out at the water's surface. "That's not far. I think we'd do just as well to go in here rather take the skiff out and go to the trouble of anchoring it."

"Maybe so," said Vansant. He stole another look at Cleo, his eyes sparkling.

"Follow me, Cleo," Casey said, wading out and fitting the mouthpiece between his teeth. When he was waist deep, he pushed out and submerged. Cleo followed, suddenly finding herself in a strange new world.

For a time her breathing was a very conscious thing as she accustomed herself to being able to breathe underwater. Ahead, Casey's flippers moved slowly up and down and a trail of pearl-like bubbles followed him. Once he looked back over his shoulder, saw that Cleo was close behind, then turned back and began to press deeper.

Cleo felt a freedom she had never before experienced, gliding along free and weightless. She swallowed and the pressure in her ears equalized.

Casey stopped and turned toward her. He pointed ahead. The boat—or what was left of it—lay there on the sandy floor of the harbor. In the pale, aquamarine light Cleo could see that the boat's superstructure had been splintered, apparently by an explosion. Drawing closer, she saw the charred decks and planking.

But the whole thing hadn't burned. Incongruously, a cotton sheet hung limply up from a shattered hole in the forward decking, waving gently as if someone were inside trying half-heartedly to signal a passer-by.

Casey paused and looked back at her. He made a signal for Cleo to wait outside while he went into the shattered hulk. She nodded and watched him as he gently moved his foot flippers and guided himself in through the opening in the bulkhead where the companionway door had been.

She waited for several seconds, then edged forward. The wreck lay heeled over on its starboard side. In the cockpit the decking was ripped up, as if by some giant hand in anger. In the semidarkness, under the deck beams, she could make out the shape of one engine.

Cleo finned across the cockpit and peered inside the shattered cabin. It was lighter here, since the entire roof had burned away except for the framework. Casey moved about looking for the charts. He saw Cleo at the companionway and motioned her away.

After a while he came out and put his hands out in a gesture that showed he'd had no success in his search. He made a motion toward the surface, but something seemed to catch his eye, and he pushed himself toward the engine compartment beneath the cockpit deck. He pulled back the smashed hatch, breaking the splintered wood about it. Wooden shards broke loose and rose from the wreckage.

Cleo's curiosity prompted her to follow him as he burrowed down into the dark opening. She moved her head to see past him, seeing his hand go out hesitantly to touch something. Looking back suddenly, he shook his head violently and motioned her away. At first she recalled some vague notion of giant octopuses lurking in the hulks of wrecked vessels, and, perversely, she moved in even closer.

And then she saw it—the lower part of a leg, a very large man's leg, protruding from between two smashed beams. Casey turned and took hold of her arms, turning her away and starting to rise toward the surface. Morbidly fascinated, Cleo looked back at the sunken boat as they both lifted toward the air.

When they broke the surface Cleo jerked the mouthpiece out. "Is there—is there really someone down there?" she asked, her tone one of disbelief.

Casey removed his mouthpiece and raised his mask. "Yeah. There's someone down there. He's wedged in behind the port engine."

"Who is it?"

"I—I didn't see his face, but I'm pretty sure it's Tiger Mobley."

Cleo gasped. *"Tiger—?"*

"Listen to me now. You go ashore and tell Vansant to call the police. I'm going back down and try to get the body out."

"But—are you certain—"

"Do as I say, Cleo," Casey said firmly. "Go on back to shore."

"I—" The previous morning's occurrence was still strong in her mind—the vitality and virility of the man. She bit her lip and nodded quickly, then turned and swam toward the shore.

After Vansant called the island constabulary, Cleo phoned the house. "Hello. Harry? We're down at the harbor. We just went down to the boat. No, the charts weren't there—at least that's not what we—what Casey found.

"I—I think you'd better come down here. The police are on the way. There was a body down there in the wreck. Yes. What? I—hold on a moment." She craned her neck and looked out the window. There was no sign of Casey yet. Vansant was pacing impatiently at the water's edge. "Harry, Casey's down there now trying to get him—trying to get the body out. He said he thinks it's Tiger Mobley."

She listened to her husband's excited voice for a while, then she said, "All right. We'll be here." Preoccupied, she lowered the phone onto its cradle.

She walked out into the bright morning sunlight. But even in the warmth of the sun she felt a chill, as if a cloud had passed over—a dark, ominous cloud.

A dozen yards out from shore Casey's head popped up. He half submerged, obviously pulling something along with him. When he reached the shallows he waded toward the shore, pulling the dead man by one arm. He turned and caught the corpse beneath the arms and backed to the edge of the water, lowered his burden, and pulled off his diver's mask.

"Stay up there, Cleo," he called. He slowly unbuckled his air tanks and lowered them to the ground beside the body. "You called the police?" he asked Vansant.

The older man nodded grimly. "I'll get a tarpaulin, Casey." He took a long look at the body. "It's Mobley. He really got it, didn't he? Looks like it blew up right in his face."

The police of St. Ursula arrived. Cleo had seen them about town, but she had come to think of them as being more in the nature of decorations for the benefit of tourists' cameras than members of a law enforcement agency. There were two of them in the car, dark men with the flat facial planes of the Arawak Indian, but doubtless with ancestry as varied as the long colonial history of the islands.

"Hello, Casey," the driver of the car said to Stribling.

"He's right down there, Rupert." Casey pointed toward the form obscured by the tarpaulin. The policeman turned toward Cleo, and Casey went on. "This is Mrs. Gregory. Constable Rupert, Cleo." He indicated the second policeman who was coming around the hood of the car. "And Constable Tambs."

"I have seen Mrs. Gregory about the village," the constable said, showing even white teeth as he grinned politely. "It is Mobley?" he asked, walking down toward the body.

Cleo looked up the road in the direction of the village, then followed the four men down the slope to the harbor's edge.

Casey looked at her with a slight frown. "This isn't a pretty sight."

"I—don't worry about me."

One of the constables lifted the canvas. The shock was not nearly as severe as Cleo had expected. Though Tiger's hair and eyebrows were burned away, the face looked almost as if he were simply in a sort of reverie, eyes half open and dull. The tarpaulin dropped over him.

"It's Mobley, all right," said Constable Tambs. "How did you happen to find him, Casey?"

As Casey began his explanation, Cleo moved back up the slope toward the building.

"Mrs. Gregory." Vansant had come up behind her and he stood with his cap in his hand. "This ain't a good way to start off a day. I got some coffee on the hot plate inside."

She looked at him frankly. "I'd much rather have a drink if you've got anything."

He grinned and nodded his head. "I've made a point of having some handy for about thirty years now! Never can tell when a snake might bite you! Come on inside."

As she took a deep swallow of the rum and water Vansant had prepared, Cleo heard the whirring sound of the Volkswagen as it pulled up outside. She went to the door just as Harry and Gene climbed out of the car.

"Cleo!" Harry strode quickly toward her. "What the devil happened? What in hell was Mobley doing—?"

Freeman punched his arm. "Harry, there are the cops down there with Stribling."

The two of them walked down to join the others. A wooden bench stood just outside the door and Cleo sat down and took another swallow of the drink.

Harry called to her. "Cleo, see if you can get in touch with Marla. Have her go to the house and keep an eye on Max."

She went inside and made the call. Marla was just closing her office with the intention of going straight to the house. One of the constables came in to use the phone just as Cleo hung up. Harry walked in behind him.

"You might as well go on back to the house yourself, Cleo. One of these boys is going to dive down to the wreck with Stribling and they want Gene and me to hang around."

"I don't suppose we'll be sailing today."

"We may. It depends on what the police say about what happened. I don't think it'll hold us up."

"Do you want me to take the car?"

Harry nodded. "We'll drive back with Stribling."

Marla and Max were sitting in the sun on the patio when Cleo arrived at the house.

"What's all the excitement?" Marla wanted to know.

"We found Tiger's body in the boat when we went down."

Marla came up from her seat. *"Tiger?"*

The reaction was almost identical to Cleo's. "That's right."

Max held the ubiquitous brandy in his hands. "So it was no accident after all, eh?"

Clo shrugged. "—I guess it wasn't."

Marla paced up and down the patio. "I can't believe it! Tiger—*dead!"*

"I didn't get much sleep last night," Cleo said. "I think I'll go to my room."

She went into the bedroom, closed the door, and lay down. For a long while she stared up at the ceiling, her mind a blank, and finally she fell asleep.

The sound of a car wakened her. Presently, the door opened and Harry looked in. "Get ready, Cleo. We're shoving off as soon as possible."

Before she could say anything the door closed. She got up and went outside. The whole group was on the patio. Harry was talking, his voice tight.

"You can't tell me that fellow was out there on his own initiative! He didn't have the brains to come in out of the rain!"

"I think you're wrong, Harry," Freeman said. "He was probably trying to find something worth stealing."

"Stribling found his body wedged in the bilge. I suppose he was stealing the damn engine?"

"I don't think Mobley was a thief," Casey put in.

Harry grunted something unintelligible and went to the table. He picked up a whiskey bottle, saw that it was empty, and sent it spinning out over the cliff. "Irene!" he yelled. "Irene!" The servant appeared in the doorway. "We're out of whiskey!" Harry snapped. "I've given you instructions! Can't you do anything the way I've told you! You lazy—"

"Leave her alone, Harry," Cleo said. "She didn't blow your boat up."

The Indian woman turned placidly and went out.

"What about this Mobley?" Max said, looking at Casey Stribling. "You say he was not the sort of fellow who would be expected to break into the boat?"

Casey shook his head. "Harry is right. Tiger would never do anything like that without someone being behind him. He was—" He put his hands out. "—well, most of you knew him. He was a man who had no idea of right or wrong, but there wasn't a malicious bone in his body. He was a—anywhere else but in St. Ursula, Tiger would probably have been in an institution. It's that simple."

Marla Keever voiced her agreement. "He was like a child, or maybe more like a dog. He'd obviously been on the short end of the stick as a fighter; probably was under the control of a bunch of thugs who didn't give a damn what they did to him, just so they made a buck. I doubt if Tiger ever did have much in the way of brains, but what he did have were thoroughly scrambled. I don't suppose anyone'll ever know just how he happened to end up down here on the island."

Gene Freeman got up when Irene brought the tray out. He poured whiskey into a glass, dropped in a couple of ice cubes. "This would all be very interesting to a group of psychology students. However, I suggest that we leave the mystery, if there is one, to the local fuzz and let's get about our business."

Cleo spoke. "The police said it was all right for us to leave?"

"We've done nothing," Harry said.

"But you said yourself somebody hired Tiger to do something. Are we all above suspicion?"

Harry gave a short laugh. "The police will only go as far as to say that he was aboard the boat without permission; that he probably did something accidentally which caused the explosion. They prefer the simple solutions to their crimes down here."

"And that's probably exactly what happened," said Freeman. "Now how about it? Is everything ready? Max, are you ready to get going?"

Heinrich nodded. "For seventeen years I have been ready, Gene."

CHAPTER NINE

IT WAS WELL AFTER NOON—almost three o'clock—when the last of the supplies and equipment had been loaded aboard the *Antares*. Nearly everything needed for the trip had been put aboard the *Belle* the previous day, and had gone down with the boat. New clothing, medication for Max, and a thousand and one other necessities had had to be replaced, making a severe dent in the few hundred dollars Harry still had.

Harry stepped aboard with the final box of canned goods and lowered the carton to the top of the trunk cabin. "How about it, Stribling? Think we've got everything we're going to need?"

Casey grinned and shook his head. "If there's something we don't have, then it's only because it's not in St. Ursula."

"Go first class whenever possible," Harry said matter-of-factly. "Even if we don't turn up this money, it's too damn late for me to start pinching pennies anyhow. I'll go to the poorhouse in a Rolls, when I go."

Freeman came up from the companionway and Harry pushed the box across the cabin top to him.

"Put that in the galley, Gene. That's the last of it."

"Put the goddamn thing down there yourself!"

Harry pulled out a pack of cigarettes and shook one out. "What's eating you?"

"You, that's what! I came to you with this thing, my old pal, cut you in and all you had to do was put up the dough! So what happens?" He swung his arm, sliding the box of supplies across the cabin top. "You go *broke!*" Freeman's eyes narrowed and he aimed a shaking finger at Harry. "We ought to cut you *out!* That's what Max and me ought to do right now, *cut you out!*"

"Knock it off, Freeman," Casey Stribling said. "The time for you two agreeing or disagreeing is long past. Now let's get this boat shipshape and shove off." He picked up the carton and stepped to the companionway. For a few seconds Freeman stood blocking the entrance, then he snorted and went below. Casey followed him down.

"That is just the beginning," Max said under his breath. Cleo, standing close to the German, was the only person who overheard him. She looked at him but he turned away and busied himself watching the harbor traffic consisting of half a dozen baggy-sailed sloops and a high-sided schooner from Barbados.

"How are you feeling, Max?" Harry said.

Heinrich did not look around. He merely shrugged and said nothing. Cleo tried to visualize him as he might have been seventeen years ago, his eye glued to the periscope, perhaps giving the orders to fire the torpedo. She could conjure up no such image of him, could not imagine him as anything but thin, bent and aged, a face and form she had seen many times selling newspapers on street corners, or standing in soup lines.

Casey came up from belowdecks. He motioned to Harry. "You've had experience with boats. Have you done any sailing?"

Harry nodded.

"Good. We'll have to divide up the duties. You'll help with the sailing. I just spoke to Freeman and he told me he sailed small boats when he was a kid, so at least he knows the fundamentals. Cleo, suit you to cook? Marla can give you a hand."

Instead of the resentment she had felt when assigned this duty aboard the *Belle,* Cleo now felt completely agreeable to the job. She smiled and nodded. "If you think you can take my cooking. I'm afraid I'm not exactly the domestic type."

"Captain Stribling." It was Max who spoke. He had taken a seat in the cockpit and was toying with the wheel. "I may be of some help, if necessary. It has been quite some time, but I was once adept at holding a boat on course."

"One of *Der Führer's* finest!" Freeman barked from the companionway.

"All right, Max," Casey said, ignoring Freeman's remark.

The lines were brought aboard and, under power, Casey eased the schooner away from the quay. He turned the wheel over to Max and, with the help of Harry and Freeman, hoisted the mainsail and the jib, and finally the foresail. The big schooner heeled over as the sails were sheeted in and the bow wave purled across the rippled surface of the harbor.

Casey took over the helm, sailed through the mouth of the harbor, and on south for a mile before coming about onto the starboard tack.

"With the wind the way it is," he said, casting an experienced glance up at the sails, "we can just about make it to the east end on this tack."

Harry looked at the chart, then handed it to Max. "I think that's where we left off. Do you agree?"

The old man regarded the chart carefully, then nodded. "It looks correct, Harry."

"Then I'd say we start right here," Casey said, touching his finger to the chart.

"I will drink to our good luck," Max said. He took a small bottle from his pocket, lifted it in a salute, and brought it up to his lips.

Harry had been standing at the mainshrouds for some time, staring out over the water. Occasionally he looked around slowly, his gaze traveling over anyone who happened to be on deck at the time.

"Want some coffee?" Cleo asked him.

He shook his head. His teeth worried at his lip and he reached out and took hold of her arm. "I've been thinking."

"So I noticed."

He overlooked the sarcasm. "Mobley wasn't trying to steal anything. Somebody hired him to fix the boat so it would blow up. That's what he was doing out there. It'd be a fairly simple matter to rig the electric bilge blower so it wouldn't work, then pour enough gasoline into the bilge to create an explosive mixture. Under those conditions, as soon as the starter button on one of the engines was pressed—" He threw his hands up descriptively. "There she'd go, along with whoever was aboard." He looked her straight in the eye. "And that would have been me."

Cleo gave him a puzzled look. "I don't understand."

"Don't you, Cleo? Don't you really? It could have been you who put him up to it."

"Could have been *me!*"

"Keep your voice down," he said, glancing around quickly. "I said it *could* have been. I didn't say it *was*."

"What on earth do I know about bilges and blowers and all that sort of thing?"

He took hold of the shrouds again. "That idiot Mobley was driving you all over the island before this happened. He had that cocker spaniel look in his eye every time you spoke to him. The damn fool would have done anything you wanted."

"You're beginning to act a little paranoiac, Harry."

"But I don't think it *was* you, Cleo. I think it was my old school chum, Mr. Eugene Freeman."

"What would he have to gain?" she wanted to know. "The whole treasure hunt almost fell through because of the boat blowing up."

"But nobody knew there was that possibility until later." He smiled strangely and his head nodded slowly. "I remember now how Gene used to try to take things away from me at school. My Old Man gave me anything I wanted —a big long convertible, the best clothes, money. I didn't live in a dorm after my freshman year; I had a damned penthouse apartment. And Gene was always conning me out of money or whiskey or using the car.

"There was this girl—" Suddenly his eyes narrowed and the muscle in his jaw knotted tightly, "—there was this girl in my senior year. I—I thought a lot of her. Gene must have known that. He started working on her, doing little insidious things that pulled her farther and farther away from me, until all of a sudden she was his." Harry's hands, gripping the shrouds, were growing white about the knuckles. "There were other times, too. He always wore a big smile, playing the original hail-fellow-well-met, but the sonofabitch had that knife in his hand."

"That was a long time ago, Harry."

"People don't change." He looked around at her quickly. "Have you noticed how he's been since it happened? For a while he was as quiet as a mouse. He wanted to let it die down because it didn't work out the way he wanted it to. And now he's turned sore—"

"Harry." It was Casey. "Give me a hand below for a couple of minutes?"

Harry released his grip on the shrouds, rubbed one hand across his face and nodded.

He started to follow Casey but Cleo touched his arm. "I don't understand—"

"Don't you?" He grinned sardonically. "Gene doesn't want just the money out of this thing." He stabbed a finger painfully against her breast. "He wants *you*." He moved past her before she could speak and disappeared down the companionway.

Puzzled, Cleo turned and stepped across the cockpit coaming. She sat down and gazed out at the jewel-like islands that dotted the surface of the sea.

A hand touched her knee. Max smiled sadly at her. "As I said before, *Liebchen,* it is only the beginning. I am afraid that few men are immune to the sickness that bothers Harry and Gene."

"The money?"

He shook his head. "That only brings it on. I'm talking about greed. At first, a share sounded all right, but now it is not enough."

"Then you think Tiger's death was an accident, that someone else was supposed to have been killed?"

"I would not make a public accusation because there is no proof." He glanced aloft at the set of the mainsail and turned the wheel slightly. "But that is what I think."

"And that's why you won't tell anybody how you marked the spot, isn't it?"

The old man frowned thoughtfully. "I would not concern myself too greatly with Harry. But Gene—He looked meaningfully at Cleo, lifted one hand and slowly drew it across his throat.

Cleo felt a chill go through her. For the first time she felt certain that there was a murderer amongst them.

Max touched her again and smiled. "Ah, *Liebchen,* forgive me. I should keep the morbid opinions of an old man to myself."

She smiled back, but without conviction.

Max adjusted himself at the wheel and leaned toward her. "Cleo—if you would—may I have just a bit of brandy? My bottle is empty."

At sunset the *Antares* bowled along, close-hauled on the long starboard tack. Astern, the sun sank behind the islands, its glow fading rapidly. The moon had already risen and stood like a huge golden ball ahead. Cleo had served sandwiches on deck for dinner. Max was below, asleep in the stateroom, and Harry was at the wheel. Freeman brooded over a folded chart.

"Where's Stribling?" Harry asked Cleo.

"Do you want him?"

"Yeah."

Casey's head appeared at the companionway. "Going to be a fine night for sailing," he said enthusiastically. He came on deck and sat on the edge of the cabin top.

"Is it safe sailing here at night?" Harry wanted to know. "What about reefs? This boat must draw quite a bit of water."

"It'll be almost as bright as day with the moon up. Just keep her on this heading and we'll be okay. I'll spell you after a while." He turned and looked up at the sails, studying the set of each of them. "Looks like that jib halyard has slacked a little." He got up and moved forward along the deck.

Cleo went below. As soon as the sun had dropped below the horizon a slight chill seemed to come on the breeze. She made her way through the galley, past Max's stateroom, through the main salon and into the forepeak where she and Harry were bunking. There were two bunks, one on either side of the thick mast which came down through the deck. *Twin beds,* she thought. *Very appropriate for us.*

She rummaged through her bag for the light sweater Casey had advised her to bring along. She found it and slipped it over her head. The soft cashmere felt good against her bare arms in the cool breeze that came into the open hatch forward of the two bunks. Cleo climbed the ladder to the hatch with the intention of closing it. But as she reached the top, she heard someone talking above.

It was Marla. "Remember, Casey," she said. "Remember when we sailed out here to Crooked Island? How long was it we stayed? A week?"

"That was a long time ago, Marla."

"There were other times, a lot of times. Back in St. Ursula. My door was never locked to you, Casey. It never will be."

"This is a business trip," Casey said. "I didn't know you were nursing Heinrich until after—well, after the deal was closed."

Her voice hardened, became brittle. "Are you saying you wouldn't have come along if you'd known I was coming?"

"Don't start trouble, Marla. Let's do this job. I'll run the boat. You look after the old man."

"I don't like getting brushed off! I can be one hell of a bitch if the occasion arises!"

"Keep your voice down. And don't act like a nagging wife—"

"A *wife!*"

Through the opening, against the moonlit sky, Cleo saw someone move.

"It's that readheaded slut!" Marla said tightly, her voice quivering. "That's who's got you so hot!"

"Cleo?" Casey said, surprise showing in his voice.

"*Cleo!* Don't forget I saw you that day at the hotel. You were looking at her like a lovesick schoolboy!" Suddenly her voice turned to honey. "Casey—we could have a good time out here. We could pick up where we left off. You haven't forgotten, have you?"

"I'd better take the wheel, Marla. Come on—"

"You bastard—"

"Somebody's coming. I'll talk to you later."

"Having trouble with that halyard, Stribling?" It was Harry's voice. "Oh—it's you, Marla."

"Who's got the wheel?" Casey asked.

"Freeman."

"I'll go on back and take a turn at it."

Cleo waited, but the prolonged silence confirmed that all three of them had gone aft. She closed the hatch and sat down on the edge of her bunk. She had thought there was something between Casey and Marla, something deeper than the friendship Stribling had admitted to.

Normally, being called a redheaded slut would have had a different effect on Cleo, but now she felt quite pleased, because Casey had not made a denial of Marla's charge.

She found herself wondering about the trip Marla had referred to, and then she found that she was putting herself in Marla's position. Just the two of them, she and Casey, aboard the schooner, sailing around the islands, the rest of the world shut out. She ran her fingers slowly over the coverlet of the bunk. Perhaps right here, on this very bed—

"Cleo," Harry stuck his head into the forepeak. "What the devil are you doing sitting up there on the bunk?" He gave her a puzzled look.. "You look like you've had a revelation!"

"I may have," she said cryptically, dropping off to the cabin floor.

"How about getting back to the galley and fixing drinks for the crowd?"

"Sure," she agreed, an enigmatic smile playing about her lips.

"No argument? No gripe? Just—just *sure?*"

"Like they say in the ads—" She reached out and touched a finger against the tip of his nose. "—sure!" Then she brushed past him and went toward the galley.

The island was a dark mass in the moonlit sea. Sails luffing in the light breeze, the schooner rounded in the cove, losing way.

"Okay!" Casey called forward. "Let the anchor go!" He turned loose the wheel and ran to the mast, loosened the halyard, and the mainsail fluttered down, the boom settling in the crutch. The foresail was next and then the jib. Casey and Harry furled the sails and, when all was shipshape, came back to the cockpit.

"Well," Casey said, looking off toward the island a hundred yards away, "we'll pick up here tomorrow morning." He dug a pack of cigarettes from his pocket, lit one. "There's a beach that goes around this cove and along the shore toward the east. Then there's a rocky cliff and another beach further around."

"You think a submarine could have come in here, among these islands?"

Casey nodded. "From what Max tells me, the skipper knew these islands well. He ran some sort of a boat down here before the war."

Harry seemed mildly surprised. "Is that so? That's more than he told me."

"I suppose everyone's hungry," Cleo said. "I'll fix something hot."

As she got the stove going and picked out the cans that were to be opened, she could not get out of her mind the conversation between Casey and Marla. The implication of what Marla had said gave her a lift and strengthened the feeling she had toward Stribling. Ever since that first day she had been drawn to him. His way of life seemed so uncluttered, so simple.

"Need any help? I'm great at KP." Freeman's mouth was very close to her ear when he spoke. She felt his breath on her neck and then his hands on her waist. "Why don't we take a little moonlight swim after dinner. We could make it over to the island and—" He moved his hands around and lifted them to her breasts.

Cleo whirled on him, her eyes flashing in the light of the lamp. "I told you to leave me alone, Gene," she hissed, throwing a quick glance toward the companionway.

"No woman ever got to me the way you have," he said thickly. "Leave him, Cleo! He's broke now. There's nothing to hold you to him! A woman like you goes where the *money* is—"

Cleo cocked her head slightly. "But he'll have money soon, Gene, won't he? Everybody will have money when Max finds this marker he's looking for."

Freeman drew in a deep breath. "Yeah. Sure." In the lamplight Cleo saw the muscles of his jaw tighten as he turned abruptly and climbed up the companionway stairs.

She opened the cans mechanically, spilling half a can of beans in her anger. As she stopped to clean the mess, someone spoke.

"Cleo." It was Casey. She turned her head and saw him standing in the doorway to the main cabin, leaning against the foot of the mainmast. "If I'm butting in, all you have to do is say so. But let me know if you need any help with Freeman, will you?"

"You—you were there? You heard him?"

He nodded.

She turned her attention back to the job, wiping up the last of the spilled food. "Thanks, Casey. I think I can handle Gene. In a way, that's sort of a synopsis of the story of my life."

He straighened and ran one hand over his short-clipped, sandy hair. "I can see how that would be true."

Suddenly coquettish, she looked askance at him, smiling. "You can?"

He grinned back at her. "I may be a sailing bum, Cleo, but believe me, I'm also human."

Seeing him standing there, smiling at her intimately, yet not with the dirt that was in Freeman's lascivious grinning, she recalled his conversation with Marla Keever. At that moment the pull was stronger than ever. The old familiar fire kindled deep within her, and she felt the heavy, forceful beat of her heart, as if in anticipation.

She took a step toward him, but a sudden hiss at the stove broke the spell and she turned back quickly to take the boiling pot off the burner.

"Thanks, Casey. Tell the others the food will be ready in a few minutes, will you?"

"Sure."

His tread was light and certain as he stepped to the companionway ladder. Cleo looked over her shoulder and watched him as he went on deck. She knew that if he ever put his hands on her, they would meet no resistance.

They ate on deck in the bright tropical moonlight, listening to music on a portable radio. The announcer spoke in Spanish, but the music was good, with the heady, sensual rhythm of the Latins.

When she finished eating, Cleo walked forward on deck and stood at the foremast, gazing out at the island. It was almost as bright as day now, the moon rising higher. The waves moved in against the shore, breaking in muffled sound and sparkling in the moonlight.

She heard a footstep nearby and saw Harry stop at the shrouds to look over at her.

"What did he say to you a while ago?"

"Who?"

"Freeman. I saw him go below when you were in the galley. He's trying to turn you against me, isn't he? He tried to kill me back there in St. Ursula, and he won't stop trying! I *know* that sonofabitch!"

"You've got no proof, Harry."

"Proof?" He laughed. "What the hell do you think this is, some kind of a TV courtroom?"

She said nothing for a moment, then inquired, "Harry? What are you going to do if we don't find this money?"

"What am I—" In the moonlight she saw him moisten his lips. "Don't be absurd, Cleo. We *will* find it. It'll—it'll just take some time, that's all."

Cleo gazed at the dark island for a moment. "I hope we do, because then I can leave you, Harry."

He turned quickly and stared at her. A knowing smile stole over his face and he shook his head. "I know you, Cleo. You might leave me, but you wouldn't leave the money."

Nine years and you don't know me at all, she thought. "I want you to watch Freeman," he told her abruptly. "All right, Harry."

She walked down the deck toward the cockpit. He wouldn't understand her reasoning in a million years. If the treasure hunt turned up nothing, she would have to stay with Harry. He would need her.

She hoped very strongly that Max would search carefully.

CHAPTER TEN

CASEY STRIBLING SAT at the wheel of the schooner, stripped to the waist, his body golden bronze in the sunlight. She was alone with him, with only the sea and the green islands and the wind filling the sails. Her heart was full as she looked into his eyes.

"Cleo..."

"Yes?"

"Cleo, wake up."

"What...?"

"I said wake up."

She opened her eyes. Against the darkness above was a rectangle of twinkling stars. A cool breeze came down the open hatch, brushing her cheek.

"Come on, Cleo. It'll be daylight in half an hour. You've got to feed this crowd."

In the pale light she made out Casey's face at the doorway.

"Let me sleep..." she mumbled, trying to close her eyes to bring back the dream. "Wanta sleep..."

He laughed, grabbed her foot and shook her. "Come on! Rise and shine!"

Someone was moving about in the other cabin. A light came on and, across the passageway, Harry yawned and sat up. Someone pumped the toilet in the head.

"I've already got coffee on," Casey said.

Marla was standing at the door to the head when Cleo joined her. "One bathroom for six people is just not enough," she said.

"I think we ought to have a rule that the men have to use the rail. Or maybe we should heed the old shipboard motto, women and children first."

"How is Max this morning?" Cleo said.

"I gave him a brandy. He's all right now. It hurts my pride a little though, sleeping in the cabin alone with a man and not having anything happen." Marla looked past Cleo. Momentarily they were alone in the main cabin. Her face grew suddenly hard. "Look, bright-eyes, Casey is mine. Is that clear? You can quit rubbing it on him, as of now!"

"I don't know what you're talking about, Marla."

"Fair warning, that's all this is. There's only one thing little Marla won't take lying down, and that's letting a big-breasted readhead take her man away—"

The door to the head opened and Freeman stepped out. "Sorry to keep you ladies waiting."

Marla brushed past him into the small room and closed the door.

"I stayed awake last night, Cleo," Freeman said. "I thought you might get lonesome. There's plenty of room in my bunk, and Stribling is clear across the boat from me."

"Very thoughtful of you, Gene."

"Keep it in mind," he said, snickering suggestively.

She finished in the head, dressed in shorts and a halter, and prepared breakfast. The sky, visible through the open companionway, was growing lighter; the stars were fading. Cleo hummed to herself as she laid strips of bacon on paper to drain, and broke eggs over the pan.

"Smells great," Casey said. He refilled his coffee mug and leaned against the bulkhead. "You're not used to keeping these hours, are you?"

She smiled and shook her head. "I think I like it, though. I—I'm beginning to like a lot of things I never knew existed." She glanced over at him. "I can see why you couldn't leave here."

His eyes grew thoughtful as he tilted the coffee cup to his lips. Finally he put it down on the counter. "I'd better start getting set for the day's work."

"Breakfast in five minutes," Cleo called after him.

Max came out of the stateroom. "Ah, *gut Morgen,* Cleo!"

"Sleep well, Max?"

"My nursemaid gave me something to make me sleep," he said with a smile.

"Want a cup of coffee?"

He opened a cabinet and took out the brandy bottle. "Perhaps later."

Breakfast was served on the gimbaled table in the main cabin. Cleo was the last to take a seat. The only place remaining was between Marla and Freeman, a seat she would not have picked voluntarily.

"Maybe today, Max?" Freeman said. He stirred more sugar into his coffee and looked across the table at Heinrich.

"It's exciting!" Marla said. She was sitting beside Harry and she turned and put her hand on his arm, glancing quickly to make certain Cleo saw her.

Br'er Rabbit and the briar patch, Cleo thought wryly.

"Hand me the bacon, Max," Harry said. He reached down the table. His hand struck against someone's coffee cup, overturning it. The hot coffee streamed across the smoothly varnished table and drained off into Freeman's lap.

"*You clumsy idiot!*" Freeman came to his feet, his eyes flashing. He reached over and grabbed Harry's shirt front. "You bastard! You did that on purpose!"

"Cut it out," Casey said with firm authority.

"Like *hell!* He's been asking for it and he's going to *get* it!" Freeman's other hand grabbed his own coffee, brought it up abruptly and threw it into Harry's face.

Casey reacted quickly as the two men tried to crawl across the table to get at each other. He pulled them apart and, seeing that Harry apparently had his emotions under control, pushed Freeman out into the galley and held him there.

Harry picked up a paper napkin and wiped the coffee off his face and neck. Marla came quickly to help him. "Thanks," he said. He crumpled the napkin and tossed it aside. "He's showing his colors now." He glanced toward the galley, a nervous smile flickering across his face. "What'd I tell you, Cleo? Huh?"

"Drop it, Harry. If you and Freeman have a bone to pick between you, wait until this thing's over." Casey stood at the galley doorway. Behind him Freeman climbed the com-

"He put that nut Mobley up to it," Harry said. "There's no doubt in my mind, not the least." He shook a finger at no one in particular. "You can mark my words, Freeman's going to cause trouble—"

Max interrupted. "We perhaps should get started?"

Harry cut his eyes toward him, then nodded. "That's right." He picked up Cleo's cup and drank the remains of her coffee. He wiped his mouth on his arm. "Let's go."

The tropical dawn came swiftly, the water of the cove turning from slate to green as the sky brightened. The boat was pulled alongside and the supplies and equipment that would be needed for the morning search were loaded aboard. Cleo got a novel from the bookshelf in the main cabin and climbed down to join the others in the boat.

"What's with the book?" Harry asked as they eased away from the schooner.

"I'm going to sit under one of those palm trees while the rest of you are off treasure hunting."

"You don't think we're going to find anything, do you?"

Cleo shrugged and looked toward the shore. "I don't know. I just don't care to come along this morning."

The boat road easily through the surf and grounded on the beach. It was pulled up clear of the tide and the few items to be taken along were divided among Marla, Freeman, Casey and Harry. Max was being treated as carefully as a queen bee.

The sun broke the eastern horizon as the group prepared to get started.

"This stretch of beach is a couple of miles long, Cleo," Casey said. "We'll try to be back for lunch." He glanced out at the anchored schooner. "The ladder's hanging over-board. If you need anything on the boat, you can swim out—"

"Come on, Stribling!" Harry said impatiently.

Cleo lit a cigarette and watched them as they moved away from the beach, Freeman swinging a machete occasionally to clear the way. In a few moments they had disappeared into the dense tropical growth. The fading sound of voices and the twack of the long knife receded gradually.

She sat down at the tall palm and laid the book on her lap. The philosophy of a beachcomber was easy to understand now. Overhead, the palm fronds rattled gently in the morning breeze; beyond the beach the schooner lay quietly at anchor in the cove, the pennant fluttering at the top of the mainmast.

She closed her eyes and smiled, feeling that she could very easily spend the rest of her life right here under this palm tree, listening to the sea birds and the soothing sound of the surf.

But it was as Casey had said, she was not accustomed to getting up so early in the morning. With a smile on her lips, Cleo went to sleep …

Her eyes popped open. The height of the sun above the horizon to her right told her she had been asleep for an hour or more. But it was not the sun that had wakened her so abruptly. To the left there was the sound of someone coming through the underbrush.

Why were they coming back so soon? Had they found something?

She was about to call out when Gene Freeman came through the thick, green foliage. He stopped when he saw her. He lifted one hand and scratched his cheek.

"I— I took a fall back there. Twisted my ankle. I thought I'd better come back to the boat and tape it up."

Her eyes went past him, and she waited. No one else had appeared out of the underbrush. "You're alone?"

He nodded, walking toward her with a slight limp. She suspected the limp had not been there earlier.

"The others—" He waved one hand in the direction from which he had come. "They're still hunting. You know how Max is, like an old woman, plodding along—"

"I'll help you get the boat in the water," Cleo said. She rose from beneath the tree, putting the book aside. When she straightened, Freeman had halved the distance between them.

"No hurry about the ankle," he said quickly. "Fact is, just walking back here on it seems to have helped. Why don't we just sit here and—talk?"

She looked at him in careful appraisal. "My guess would be you didn't twist your ankle at all, Gene. I think you came back here with some wild idea about your irresistible charm having the desired effect on me. I think—"

"You think too much." He moved quickly, closing the gap between them, his hands gripping her forearms. But she was not unprepared. She turned quickly and broke the hold. They stood face to face, each waiting to see what the other would do.

Freeman's eyes blinked rapidly. "Cleo—"

She stepped back, trying to get the tree between them.

He shook his head. "You damned bitch! I can't sleep thinking about you! I sprawled there in that bunk last night, knowing you were just on the other side of the bulkhead. I listened, trying to hear you breathe, praying you'd get up when Harry went to sleep and come in there with me." He moved forward slowly, his feet dragging through the sand. "I can't think of a damn thing but you! I want to run my hands through your hair, feel that body against me—"

He lunged. Cleo threw herself to the side, but his clawing fingers caught on the halter she wore, ripping it away, baring her breasts. He stared at her, the piece of ripped cloth dropping unnoticed from his hand. His eyes were on her breasts as they rose and fell with her quickened breathing. His nostrils widened and he moistened his lips.

"I'm going to have you, Cleo, one way or another. One way or *another*—"

He threw his body at her in a flying tackle. Alert as she was, his lightning-like move was too fast for her. His arms darted around her waist, carrying her to the earth. She fought silently, trying to get her knee up, but Freeman anticipated her move and clung tightly to her.

"Don't fight it," he said between clenched teeth. "Come on, baby—*give a little.*"

One hand reached down for her shorts. His fingers slipped beneath the waistband and, with a sudden jerk, tore down the side. His splayed fingers slid across her buttocks, caressing the soft, contoured flesh. His mouth pressed against her face, seeking her lips.

Cleo tried desperately to bite him, but he pulled his other hand up, clutched his fingers in her hair and jerked her head back against the ground.

"You want it like this," he rasped, "you get it like this..."

She heard the rip of cloth and knew the shorts were gone. His knee rammed between her legs, forcing her thighs apart, his body an oppressive weight bearing down on her.

Cleo beat at him with her fists, tried to claw him with her nails, but there was no room for leverage and the blows rained ineffectively against his back.

Everything seemed to turn red before her eyes, and she realized that Freeman's shoulder was pressing down hard against her throat. She was blacking out. She squirmed, tried to scream. Her strength seemed to wane and, for a terrifying instant, she wondered if perhaps he was going to kill her. Perhaps he had gone completely mad.

She tried to draw in her breath, but all his weight was against her now. In her ear Freeman's breathing grew heavy and ragged.

As if at a great distance, she heard him yell, and then a great soothing mass of air rushed into her lungs, sweeping away the darkness. She gulped in the air, marveling at the wonder of this simple act that was usually taken for granted.

Her eyes opened; immediately she saw what had happened. Casey Stribling held Freeman at arm's length with one hand, while his other formed a fist and came around to smash against Freeman's jaw. He fell back, taking Casey with him. Freeman cursed and jerked his right knee up, the blow glancing off Casey's thigh. They rolled over and down onto the beach, both trying for advantage.

Cleo tried to pull herself up, but everything seemed to tilt precipitously and she fell back. She heard the sound of hard flesh striking flesh. Freeman cursed again, then screamed in pain. Cleo turned her head, feeling her equilibrium returning.

She saw Freeman trying to break the grip Casey had about his neck. There was a ripping of cloth, and Freeman spun away, his shirt hanging in shreds. His feet dug at the sand and he scrambled up the slight embankment, flinging himself into the brush.

Casey was close behind him, but he stopped short, rubbing his knuckles as he looked after the vanishing form of Freeman. He climbed the slope and dropped on one knee beside Cleo.

"Are you all right?"

"I—don't know—" She rubbed her throat and tried to sit up. Casey leaned forward and slipped an arm under her shoulders, helping her up. She smiled at him and lifted one hand to his face, "Your—your nose is bleeding."

"You ought to see the other guy," he said.

She moved the hand to her hair, brushing it back. "How did you hapen to get here? The—cavalry to the rescue. In the nick of time, as they say."

"When Freeman said he'd twisted his ankle and wanted to come back to the boat to see about it, I remembered last night. So I came back, too. I told the others I'd have to find the tape for Freeman."

"I—" Cleo glanced down, realizing suddenly that she was completely naked, that Freeman had torn both her shorts and her halter off.

Casey pulled his arm from behind her. He made a flustered effort to look away. Then, with a quick motion, he pulled his shirt over his head and handed it to Cleo.

"He won't be back. I'll row out to the boat and get you some clothes." He started to rise but Cleo reached out impulsively and put her hand on his forearm.

"Casey..." she faltered, looking at him, invitation in her eyes. It was like a sudden, unexpected continuation of the dream which had been interrupted that morning. "Casey —I—"

"I'd better go—"

Almost as if he were fighting against it, he moved back toward her. He touched the hand that lay on his arm, his fingers brushing over hers lightly, as though trying to determine if they were really there.

"I'm—I'm a little short on will power, Cleo."

"I hoped you would be," she said, smiling now, more sure of herself.

He knelt before her on the sand. The shirt had dropped, forgotten. He took her face gently in both hands and looked into her eyes. "Ever since that first day when you tied up behind my boat at the quay, I haven't been able to get you out of my head." His fingers moved over her cheeks, went down to her neck, across her shoulders. She moved against him eagerly, her own arms reaching around him, pulling him hard against her.

"Casey! Casey!"

"When a man gets a woman on his mind, it's rough on him, Cleo. Particularly if she's married."

What a time jar high principles, she thought. She lifted her face to him, brushing her lips tantalizingly against his. His arms tightened, pulling her against him, her breasts pressing against the hard expanse of his chest. The hunger inside Cleo rose, swelling and overwhelming. Her lips parted under his kiss, her tongue darting inside his mouth.

His hands moved eagerly over her naked body. He lowered her back against the earth, his mouth moving from hers, across her cheek, to her neck and then against her breast, toying with the hard round nipple.

"Casey..." she breathed, finding it an effort to speak. She drew her arms tight about him. "Casey—stay this way always. Don't ever leave me..."

"Cleo..." She could still feel his heart pounding heavily against her breast. "It's never been like this before." She nibbled at his ear. "Not with anybody. Not even Marla."

She pulled his face to hers and kissed him. She had found him, she knew that now. She had found the man for her. With a great surge of strength he found her and she hooked her legs together about him, giving herself up entirely to the fierce rapture of the moment.

When they had had their fill of each other Casey raised himself and moved away. He picked up the shirt from the ground, took a pack of cigarettes from the pocket. He lit two and placed one between Cleo's lips.

"I hope the others never come back," Cleo said dreamily. "I hope they walk right off the end of the island."

He laughed silently. "They'll be back. And I think you'd better have some clothes on when they do." He got up and - went to the boat, dragging it across the sand to the water. "What do you want me to bring you?"

Cleo sat up, then stood, brushing sand from her body. Her knees felt weak, but she dropped the cigarette and ran down the beach to the water. She swam to the schooner and climbed the boarding ladder. By the time Casey pulled alongside in the skiff, she was below and nearly dressed.

He was standing in the skiff, his hand on the mainshroud. "Hop in."

Cleo smiled at him and climbed down into the boat. She sat in the stern and, as he pulled away toward the shore, said, "Casey . .

"Yes?"

"I'm glad. I'm glad it happened."

He grinned at her as he pulled easily on the oars. "I am, too."

And then, in this moment of contentment, she thought of Freeman and of what Harry had said about him. He was not a man who would take the humiliation he had just received, not without striking back.

Her eyes scanned the beach. There was no one about. Only the sand and the jungle and the blue sky above it all.

CHAPTER ELEVEN

THE ATMOSPHERE ABOARD the *Antares* seemed charged with electricity. Cleo found herself unable to keep either her thoughts or her eyes off Casey. Three days had gone by since the incident on the beach; days that were filled with longing for Cleo; nights alive with desire and remembering Casey's touch, knowing he was there in the darkness only a few feet from where she lay in her bunk.

Harry, almost fully occupied with thoughts of the treasure, still had perception enough to sense something different about Cleo. After that came suspicion and he watched, first Cleo and Freeman and then Cleo and Stribling, looking for telltale signs which might give him a lead. Slowly it began to dawn on him that the relationship between Stribling and Cleo had grown, somehow, as if they'd known each other for years and were able to sit without talking, content in each other's presence, even though at opposite ends of the schooner. That intimacy aroused his anxiety and he was prompted to speak about it one day after catching fleeting, warm smiles, full of remembrances and promises, darting between them.

Cleo stared at him unabashed, her manner indicating that she thought he was out of his mind. Unsure of himself, the lack of success in the treasure hunt uppermost in his mind, he gave in, determined not to start something he couldn't finish.

Freeman, too, sensed something different but, having been caught out by Casey in attempted rape, he had to be content with glaring at his frustrater and turning antagonistic toward everyone. He cursed Max for being slow, accused him of deliberately delaying the search, though his reasoning behind this was vague and cloudy.

Harry's fear of Freeman grew with each day and, at night, he would not go on deck alone unless he knew where Freeman was. The two spoke only when it became absolutely essential to the work at hand.

Each day the search went on for Max's marker, and the close of each unsuccessful day's hike brought with it shortened tempers and heightened conflict.

The fourth morning found the schooner lying off a beach in the lee of a steeply hilled island. The sun had risen, but no preparations were being made for going ashore. It had been decided to let Max rest and to pick up the search in the afternoon.

"There's a fresh water spring just beyond the beach there, Cleo," Casey said. "Are you tired of salt water baths?"

"Sounds fine," she said.

"Get your stuff together and I'll row you ashore."

She went below, got a bar of soap and gathered together a few items of clothing to wash.

"Where're you going?" Harry wanted to know.

She told him about the spring and he nodded sullenly, vaguely troubled but still determined not to get into a quarrel while he was still at a disadvantage.

Casey had the boat alongside when she came on deck and lie rowed her to shore. Cleo stepped out in the shallows.

"Right across that hill," Casey said, pointing "You can't miss it."

"You're sure there're no snakes?"

He grinned and shook his head. "The only snake around is our friend Gene, and I'll make sure he stays aboard the *Antares* while you're ashore."

She looked toward the schooner. They were all on deck, Max sitting in his usual place at the foot of the mainmast, Marla and

Harry in the cockpit. Freeman stood at the shrouds, watching the two people at the edge of the beach.

Cleo turned back to Casey. "I—I wish you could come with me."

"There's nothing on earth I'd like better," he said. "Cleo, I—"

"Yes?"

He ran his fingers quickly over his chin. "Nothing. Give me a shove off. I'll watch for you when you're done."

She pushed the skiff away and waded ashore, looking back once, then climbing the slope from the beach.

A five-minute walk brought her to the spring, just as Casey had predicted. Water dropped from a cleft in the mossy rock of a steep hillside; a pool formed beneath the flow and the resultant stream pushed its way through thick growths of fern and disappeared.

Cleo found a smooth, flat rock at the edge of the pool and arranged her things. She sat down, lit a cigarette and looked about her. The place had a primeval air about it, as if she had been thrust back millions of years in time. There was only the sound of the water and the wind in the trees, high up on the hillside.

A plant with huge red blossoms hung out over the water on the opposite side of the pool. She took a final draw on the cigarette and flipped it into the pool, feeling, as she did, that the act had been a minor sacrilege. Unhurriedly she removed her clothes, folding them and placing them on the rock.

Naked, the effect of being taken back in time became even stronger. It was as if she were some primitive woman, with all the veneer and the artificiality wiped away.

She thought of Casey, no more than a quarter of a mile away. *If he were only here now.* She spread her fingers over her stomach, pressing against the hollow longing inside.

She waded into the water, taking up the bar of soap and began to lather her body. The sun filtered down through the trees, warm against her skin. She put the soap back on the rock and pushed herself out to the center of the pool. With her feet on the sandy bottom, the water came just to her breasts. She lay back and floated, looking up at the bright sky. This was what she wanted, to stay here in the islands for the rest of her life.

Her feet sank and she stood again. A startled cry escaped her as she looked toward the bank of the pool.

"It's just me," Marla said. "Who were you expecting? Casey?" She pulled her blouse over her head and dropped it to the ground. Then she stepped out of her shorts, revealing a well-proportioned body.

"I wasn't expecting anyone," Cleo answered, trying to contain her sudden feeling of anger. "That's why you startled me."

Marla paused in the shallows and squatted, splashing water over her body. She began to lather herself. "What happened the other day between you and Freeman? He acts like he's got a loose screw, glaring and snapping at everybody the way he does."

"What makes you think I've got anything to do with the way he acts?"

"It started that day he said he twisted his ankle. I've noticed the ankle mended marvelously, but his disposition hasn't"

"Maybe it's because Max hasn't found the money yet."

Marla made a derisive sound. "It's little Miss Hotpants who's got him the way he is! Yes, and my Casey, too!"

"You're imagining things," Cleo said, dismissing it.

"Like hell I am! Casey and I had a—we had a very good relationship before you came along."

"Quite a while before I came along, the way I see it."

"Maybe so, but he would have come back to me," She tossed the cake of soap aside. "How old are you, Cleo? Twenty-five? Twenty-eight, at the outside. You've got a good ten years on me, that's to your advantage. But I've got determination on my side, honey. I never give up without a fight, and I can fight dirty when I have to."

"Oh, for God's sake, Marla, shut up!" Cleo ducked under, rinsing her body in the cool fresh water, then she waded out and picked up the towel.

Her back was turned toward Marla. She heard a sudden splash behind her and felt the impact of Marla's body smashing into her.

"You thieving bitch!" Marla screamed.

Cleo's surprise was total. The momentum of the other woman's tackle carried them both across the ground, sending them crashing into the tall ferns about the pool.

Cleo's fall was cushioned somewhat by the thick leaves, but Marla fell astride her, her wet body slick with soap from her bath. She screamed obscenities at Cleo, her hands grasping in Cleo's hair and banging her head against the earth.

"Stop it, Marla!" Cleo tried to squirm from beneath the enraged woman, but Marla planted her knees against the ground, bracing herself, pressing all her weight down on Cleo's stomach. Cleo brought her arms up, trying to break Marla's grip on her hair.

The pain caused her to cry out and, in desperation ,she swung her right hand wide, balling it into a fist, catching Marla on the chin. The blow snapped the big woman's head to the right, her grip on Cleo's hair slackening. Cleo twisted violently and they both tumbled over in the undergrowth.

She saw Marla scrambling toward her on all fours, her eyes blazing. Cleo leaped to her feet and moved away quickly, putting several yards between them.

"Marla! Stop it! There's no sense to this!"

Marla was on her feet now, her body tensed, feet apart. "I'm going to teach you something, doll! I'm going to teach you what happens to little girls who go around stealing men who don't belong to them!"

She started forward warily, her naked body gleaming and soapy, with fern leaves and earth sticking to her from the thrashing about on the ground. Seeing that Cleo was not moving back, she ran toward her, only to find herself going down, with the aid of a clumsy judo hold Cleo had learned from Harry.

"Let's get cleaned up, Marla," Cleo said, "and go back to the boat. This is foolish—"

But the older woman was far from ready to give up. She got up silently, her eyes glaring with hatred, her nostrils flared. As she moved, her heavy breasts jarred with each step.

Suddenly she lashed out at Cleo with her nails extended and, as Cleo tried to turn her face away, Marla stepped close and threw her arms around the smaller woman.

Again they fell to the ground, scratching and snarling like cats. They rolled back and forth, first one on top and then the other, crashing about in the underbrush. Momentarily the hold between them was broken and Cleo sprang to her feet, only to have a screaming Marla grasp her ankles and bring her down again. Both kicked and twisted, each trying to inflict as much pain as possible on the other.

Minutes passed. What the fight now lacked in vigor was made up for in determination. Both were obviously tiring. Their breathing grew stertorous and painful as they slapped, gouged and twisted. With a great effort, Marla rolled over suddenly, and Cleo found herself falling into the pool, the coolness of the water like a balm against her flesh.

She was free of the other woman for the moment but, as she started to rise, she saw that Marla had come to her feet and was standing at the edge of the pool with a large, round stone in her hands, upraised above her head. Her eyes glittered, her lips were drawn back wolf-like over her teeth. There was no way for Cleo to escape now; she had no strength left with which to avoid the blow that was coming.

But the stone hung there above Cleo for what seemed like an eternity. Then, swaying with frustration, Marla moved the stone forward and released it. It fell with a heavy splash, harmlessly, just at the edge of the pool.

"I—I couldn't do it—" Marla muttered sheepishly.

She dropped, exhausted, and rolled over into the pool. Realizing the fight was gone out of both of them, Cleo sank down again into the cool water.

They said nothing to each other as they came out of the water, dried themselves carefully, dressed, and made their way back to the beach.

Casey rowed ashore to pick them up. "We've decided to take the whole day off," he said, pulling on the oars. He looked curiously at both of them, his eyes lingering on a ruddy bruise high on Cleo's cheek. But he continued as if there had been no pause in his speech. "At least, that's what Harry and I agreed on. You can't get Freeman to agree on anything."

"It'll do the old man a lot of good to rest," Marla said.

"You know that little fishing village on Crooked Island?"

Marla smiled and nodded. "I know it."

Cleo recalled the conversation between them and Marla's mention of Crooked Island. She felt a sudden pang of jealousy.

Casey eased the skiff alongside the schooner and took hold of the gunwale. "It's only a couple of hours' sail from here, and we can get fresh meat there. Maybe we can find some milk for the old man."

Cleo went below, beginning to feel the bruises Marla had inflicted. Strangely, she felt no animosity toward the other woman. As she stowed the still unwashed clothes away, she knew that if she were losing Casey, she would fight, too.

When she returned topside, the sails were up and Casey and Harry were forward, bringing in the anchor. Max sat at the wheel.

"Where's Freeman?" she asked him.

"He is below, perhaps in the head. Here, come sit with me.

She sat down in the cockpit beside the German. She took a pack of cigarettes from her pocket and lit one. "Are you becoming discouraged, Max? Have you thought that maybe this—this marker of yours may have disappeared after all this time?"

He closed his eyes and shook his head slowly. "It has not disappeared, and neither has the money. It is all there, waiting patiently." He opened his eyes into narrow slits. "We could use some of that aboard this schooner—patience."

"Max!" Casey yelled back from the bow. "Crank up the engine, Max! Ease her forward; the anchor's fouled on the coral!"

He turned the switch beneath the seat and the auxiliary engine came purring to life. He pushed the gear lever down and the boat moved forward slowly.

"We narrow it down each day," Max said. "We will find it."

"And what happens then?" Cleo mused.

"Ah—you have thought of that also! I do not know. Already it is bad and it grows worse. Gene and Harry do not speak. Gene glares at the captain as if he would cut his throat."

"Yes," Cleo said thoughtfully. "I know."

Forward, Harry waved his hand. "Got it, Max! Anchor's clear!"

Max cut the engine and eased the wheel down. The mainsail, already sheeted in, filled and the schooner heeled lazily under the light air in the lee of the island.

The village on Crooked Island spread out at the foot of tall green hills, along the shore of a well-protected bay. Cleo had vaguely expected a few huts, but there were quite a number of houses along the beach, and a rickety wharf poking out into the bay.

The sails were lowered as the schooner entered the bay and, under auxiliary power, Casey brought the boat alongside the wharf. He was no stranger to the dozen or more people who greeted them. As soon as the boat was tied up Casey and Harry went ashore with one of the men who had met them.

"A waste of time," Freeman grumbled. He put one foot on the cockpit coaming and looked at Max, who was sitting at the base of the mainmast with his brandy in his hand. "Look at him! Just *look* at him!

"Sitting there like a bloody yachtsman at a regatta! "

"He's tired," Marla said.

"Why don't you sit down and relax," Cleo said, lowering the book she had begun to read. "Or better yet, go ashore."

Freeman glared at her. He seemed about to say something but he savagely smacked his fist into his open palm and went clattering down the companionway.

"Something bothers Gene," Max said in a monotone. "I have read of men who hunt for treasure. Sometimes they go—" He lifted one hand and made a slowly circling motion at his temple.

Freeman reappeared at the companionway, a bottle in one hand and a glass in the other. "Look, you lousy kraut, if it wasn't for *me*, you'd still be cooling your heels in the old country!"

"No offense, Gene," said the old man, leaning back against the mast and taking a swallow of his brandy. "We all become a bit—what is the word?" Then he chuckled quietly. "Greedy?"

"To hell with you!" Freeman barked angrily. He climbed off onto the wharf. "To hell with the whole lot of you! "

He stalked across the wharf, turned and went a hundred yards up the beach where he sat down beneath a tall palm and stared broodingly at the bay, throwing an occasional glance at those aboard the schooner.

The two men returned with a gallon of milk and several fresh vegetables which Cleo put in the galley. The afternoon passed slowly. It was as if they were in a waiting room somewhere, watching the time go by with agonizing slowness.

Max remained almost immobile in the shade of the deck awning that was hoisted above the main boom for protection from the fierce heat of the sun. He drank brandy steadily and at times seemed to drift off to sleep. Once, Marla tried to get him to go below to his bunk.

He shook his head. "I will stay here on deck."

"It's hot below, this time of day," Casey said. "Maybe he'll be better off out here."

Cleo prepared dinner with only moderate success. No one seemed hungry. She sent Max's plate topside to him and, when everyone was finished, Casey volunteered to take the dirty dishes on deck and wash them. She cleaned up the galley and went up to the cockpit. Casey was sitting on the coaming, the pail of dishwater before him.

"A very domestic scene," Cleo observed with a smile.

Casey glanced at her, his eyes steady on hers. "It makes you think."

"Casey— Casey, I think when this is over—"

Harry came on deck. "Have either of you seen Max?"

"Not in the last fifteen minutes or so," Cleo said. "Why? I thought he went to his cabin. He wouldn't eat much."

Freeman appeared out of the darkness on the wharf. He drew on his cigarette, the tiny coal lighting his face. "He's off drunk somewhere."

"You've seen him?"

"No, but it's simple to figure. He's been sucking on that brandy since sunup."

Marla came up the companionway. "I thought he was with you, Gene—"

"Where in the name of God did you get that idea?" he snapped.

"I saw him on deck with you, didn't I?"

"No, you *didn't* see me on deck with him! When I finished eating I took a little walk in the village. Christ, but these people turn in when the sun goes down."

"You haven't seen him?" Casey said.

"I just told you. What the hell *is* this? Every time the goddamn boat rocks you all look at *me!* Well, I'm getting tired of it! I'm getting very *goddamn* tired of it!" He flicked the butt of his cigarette across the deck and into the bay.

"We'd better look for him," Casey said, interrupting the tirade.

Freeman took hold of a shroud and swung aboard. "Screw the kraut. Let him find his own way back."

Harry rubbed a hand quickly through his hair and glanced down the dark beach. "If anything happens to Max—"

"We'll all look for him," Marla put in.

"Well," Freeman said, reluctance in his voice, "if we've got to look for him, we'd better split up."

Cleo thought she saw Harry dart his eyes toward Freeman. It was strange, the way Freeman was taking Max's disappearance. Knowing Max was the key, the only key, she would have expected Freeman to be in the vanguard of the search, the most worried member of the group. Instead, he was almost disinterested.

"All right." Casey said. "Marla, you go through the village. Ask around. Maybe somebody's seen him."

"If you can find anybody awake," said Freeman.

"Harry, you go along the beach to the left. I'll go to the right." Casey looked directly at Freeman. "Do you want to help, Gene?"

Freeman shrugged. "Nothing else to do."

"Okay. You go with Marla. You take the left side and Marla the right. I'll go up the beach to the right."

"What about me?" said Cleo.

"You wait here. If he comes back, keep him here."

She nodded and watched the four go off into the night, the flashlights of Casey and Harry moving up the edge of the beach. It was odd. It was not at all like Max to wander off. He had always been very content to sit quietly with his brandy.

Suddenly, she got up, climbed onto the wharf and ran ashore. She turned to the right as she reached shore and went down the beach. The moon would not rise for another hour, and the island lay like a dark, sleeping giant on one side of her, the bay a black void on the other. The beach was a pale strip before her.

"Who's there?" a voice called.

"Casey? It's Cleo. Where are you?"

A flashlight snapped on. "Right here. What is it? Did he come back?"

"No, I—" She stopped before him. He snapped the light off. "Casey, there's something—something odd about this. Max wouldn't just wander off, drunk or sober."

She felt his hand touch her cheek and her heart leaped. But he pulled the hand away and snapped the light on again, shining it down the beach in the direction of the village.

"Did you hear something?" he said.

"No ... " She turned and watched the beam of light play along the edge of the jungle. The small waves of the bay whispered against the sand.

After a moment, Casey said, "I think you're right. There's something a little fishy about this. Let's head back. There's a pathway through there." He aimed the light at the edge of the beach. "It leads around back of the village. We'll take a look and then I'll rout out a few people I know to help search for him, if he hasn't been turned up by the others."

Cleo followed him up the beach and onto the narrow pathway. She kept close to him, with the odd and uncomfortable sensation that they were not alone, that there was someone in the darkness behind them.

"Hurry, Casey," she said. But there was a sudden rustle of leaves back of her, and then something struck against her head, a blow that seemed to jerk the strength out of her entire body. As she fell, she seemed to hear another blow, and the sound of a voice, but she was unable to do anything against the sweeping blackness that settled over her.

"Cleo ... ?"

She opened her eyes. Directly above her were the deck beams of the schooner. She turned her head and saw that she was on the bed in the main cabin.

Casey stood beside the bunk. "Cleo?" he said again. "I think she's coming around."

She looked up at him. He wore no shirt. White gauze was wrapped about the upper part of his right arm and across his shoulder. A sling about his neck supported the arm.

"What—what happened?" she asked weakly.

Harry came to stand beside Casey. "Somebody jumped you two. It's a good thing you were near the village. One of the fishermen heard the noise and came out. The way it looks, you were hit on the head and he—whoever it was—had a knife. Stribling got a pretty nasty cut."

"Who was it?" She lifted herself on one elbow, allowed the sudden dizziness to pass, and sat up on the edge of the bunk.

"Here," Marla said, handing her a glass. "Drink this."

She accepted the glass and took a swalllow. It was whiskey, straight, and it brought tears to her eyes.

"Don't know who it was," Marla said.

"Some of these no-good natives," Freeman put in.

"But why?"

"There's no way of finding out who it was," Casey said. "So let's let it drop."

It was someone who's in this cabin right now, Cleo told herself. Her eyes went around the room, stopping on Harry's face, impassive in the lamplight. Freeman, lounging against the bulkhead, seemed to be almost drunk. She turned to face Marla. Briefly their eyes locked, both remembering the fight at the pool that morning. It could have been any of them. They'd all been separated while searching for Max. *Max!*

"What about Max?" she said.

Marla nodded her head toward the door to the stateroom. "He's in there now. He was right under the wharf all the time, passed out."

"Under the wharf? How did he get under there?"

"How the hell would anybody get under there?" Freeman said. "He walked."

"But—" Cleo started to say.

"I think we'd all better turn in," Casey interrupted. "We'll try to shove off early tomorrow morning if Max is up to it. The best thing we can do now is wind up this job, and do it as soon as possible."

A sudden vagary of the night wind moved the schooner—the mooring lines groaned as if in agreement with Casey's argument.

CHAPTER TWELVE

HE SOUND OF VOICES woke Cleo. The forepeak was dark, but light filtered in from the main cabin. Across from her, Harry's bunk was empty.

Cleo threw back the sheet and got out of bed. In the main cabin, Harry stood in his pajamas at the open door of the stateroom. Freeman stood beside him, craning to get a look through the doorway.

"What's wrong?" Cleo asked, rubbing her sleep-swollen eyes.

"Max," Harry said without turning. "He's had some kind of attack."

"You mean somebody—"

"No, no!" He glanced around quickly. "Marla says it's his heart."

She went to the door, pushed past the two men and went into the small stateroom. Casey and Marla were there at the side of Max's bunk, Marla administering something with a hypodermic needle.

Casey turned and saw Cleo. He gave a little shrug.

"Wait outside," Marla said. "I'll call if I need you. Both of you."

They went out to join Harry and Freeman.

"What about it, Stribling?" Freeman said brusquely. "How does it look?"

"You know as much as I do. Marla says it's a heart attack. It looks like a bad one."

"He'll die?" Freeman asked, his voice tinged with anger. "Did she say he might die?"

"Go sit down someplace," Casey said disgustedly.

"You can't tell me what to do! I've got as much right to know what's going on in there as anybody here!"

"Gene," Harry said. He seemed to make an effort to contain himself. "Gene, for now, will you just calm down?"

Freeman took hold of Harry's arm, and for a moment it seemed that they might come to blows. But he wanted to talk. "Harry, you've got as much at stake as I have. I say you and I should forget our differences and face up to this thing. That old man in there—" He waved a finger menacingly at the stateroom. "—that old man is the only one who knows where the dough is. If he dies, the whole shebang goes down the drain. There won't be a thin dime to divide." He leaned toward Harry's ear. "We've got to make him talk. We've *got* to, Harry! We've been too damned easy on him!"

Harry tried to pull away. He moved into the galley, but Freeman clung to him.

"Nobody's going in there with Max now," Casey said firmly.

"Listen to him, Harry," Freeman went on. "It's the two of us against him! What'll you do if we don't get that money? Do you know what it is to be a poor man, Harry? No, you don't! You won't like it, my friend! I can tell you that much—"

"*Shut up!*" Harry exploded, pushing him away and jerking up the bottle of Scotch from the galley. He poured a stiff drink into a glass and turned it up to his mouth.

"Should we sail back to St. Ursula, Casey?" Cleo asked.

"I don't know. I'd say we ought to leave that up to Marla. She's the nearest thing to a doctor we've got."

"Maybe there's a radio transmitter here on the island," Harry conjectured. "We could call Heath—"

"Forget it. These people see the mail boat once every two weeks. That's their only contact with the outside world, except when they go to St. Ursula themselves."

The stateroom door opened and Marla stepped out. Her face was tired and expressionless. "Max is a very sick man," she said to them.

"You can do better than that," Freeman told her. *"How* sick is he? Is he dying?"

"He can hear you, Gene!" Harry whispered harshly.

"No," Marla answered. She picked up a pack of cigarettes from the table and lit one. "He's asleep." She took a deep drag and her face darkened. "Heath didn't foresee this. The fact is, the stuff he prescribed for Max may have brought this on, to a degree."

"To hell with what's done!" Freeman said hotly. "What happens now?"

"We wait." She turned toward Casey. "How's the wound?"

He shrugged. "Okay. It's a little inconvenient having my arm in this sling, though."

"When will he wake up?" Freeman went on. "Harry and I want to talk to him."

"You're not going to badger that old man!" Marla said, glaring at Freeman.

"Maybe we should get him back to the doctor," Cleo suggested.

Marla turned to Casey. "She's right. How soon can we sail?"

"Right now," He glanced at his watch. "It's nearly five. The way the wind is we'll have it on the quarter all the way to St. Ursula. It ought to take—" He paused, calculating. "—eight to ten hours."

Cleo gave him a puzzled look. "That long?"

Casey smiled. "This isn't like that cruiser you people had. The old girl knocks along at five or six knots and that's it." He turned and headed through the galley. "Harry, you and Freeman come on topside. Let's shove off."

Through the hours of dawn, as the sun lifted slowly over the horizon astern, the *Antares* corkscrewed along under the quartering wind and sea. An uncomfortable quiet had settled over the boat, as all were vaguely aware of some strange malevolent power at work against them and their mission.

Cleo served a breakfast of sandwiches and coffee in the cockpit and took Marla's food to her in the cabin where she kept a vigil on Max.

Cleo ate her own breakfast in the cockpit, where Harry briefly spelled Casey at the wheel. Freeman stood on the fantail, sullen, glowering at anyone who ventured to speak to him.

Marla appeared at the companionway. "Cleo." She beckoned with her hand.

Cleo hastened to put her sandwich aside, following Marla down the companionway. In the galley, Marla paused. "He's asking to see you," she said.

"Me?" Cleo said.

"He's dying, Cleo. Don't keep him waiting." She stepped aside, allowing Cleo to pass.

Max lay on the narrow bunk in the stateroom, his face more drawn than ever, his eyes sunk deep in the sockets. Except for the flicker of his eyes as he turned them toward Cleo, he could easily have been taken for dead already.

"Max?" Cleo said, whispering. She could hear water rushing along the hull beyond the old man.

"*Liebchen...*" The skeletonlike hand at his side moved.

She came and sat on the edge of the bunk, smiling down at him. "Now you rest, Max. No more hiking around these islands for a long time, do you understand?"

His eyes went past her and he nodded toward the door. "Close it..."

She got up and silently shut the door. She took her seat beside him again. "Can I get you something? Is there anything you'd like me to do to make you more comfortable?"

"You are kind, Cleo. You—are very—kind. That is important..." His eyes drooped, closed, and he began to speak very softly in his native tongue. After a moment he roused somewhat. "I—want you to know how I marked the —cache—"

"Are you sure you want to do this?" she said earnestly. "Please be certain, Max."

His head gave a little nod. "I am certain." Again he looked past to the closed door. "There are—rocks. Cross—a cross—two meters in each direction—" He paused, his breathing rapid and shallow, as though the few words had tired him.

"It's buried beneath the cross?" Cleo asked.

He shook his head feebly. "While the—seamen buried the money—I made the marker—" His fingers sought her hand. The touch of his flesh was cold. "Twenty paces—directly toward the beach—toward the North Star—"

The cabin door opened and Marla poked her head in. Max nodded to Cleo, smiled and closed his eyes. His hand fell away from hers and she stood up.

Marla came to the side of the bunk and lifted his wrist. She held it for a moment in her fingers.

"Is he—is he dead?" Cleo whispered.

"No. Not quite."

The boat took a sudden heel and both women grabbed for support.

"Is there anything more you can do for him?"

Marla shook her head. She lowered his hand and sighed. "I kinda liked the old boy, you know?"

Cleo turned toward the door. "I know." She went out and closed the door behind her.

In the galley, Freeman grabbed her by the shoulders. "How is he? Did he—did he tell you anything?" His eyes gleamed. His face seemed to shine, as if he were perspiring.

Cleo looked at him for a moment, then she shook her head. "No. He wasn't conscious."

Freeman jerked his hands away and slammed his palm down against the counter top. "He's going to *die* without telling us how to find that goddamn money! The lousy sonofabitch is going to *die!*"

Harry came down the companionway. "How is he?"

"He's dying," Cleo said, her voice hushed.

Freeman's wildly swinging arms froze. He looked quickly toward the stateroom door. "Oh, no, he's not! He's not going to do that to *me;* not to Gene Freeman! I'll wring it out of him!" His voice rose. "I'll choke it out of him! *He'll tell me or, by God, he'll wish he was dead—!*"

The door opened slowly. Marla Keever stepped out, closed the door behind her, and with a tired motion pushed back the strands of hair that hung over her forehead.

"He doesn't have to wish he was dead, Gene." she said in a monotone. She looked at Harry, then at Cleo. "He just died."

Freeman's mouth hung open. A glistening cord of spittle ran slowly from the corner of his mouth. "No, *no!*" A shaking finger came out and aimed pistol-like at Marla. "You're trying to keep it to yourself. You've got him in there; you've got him doped up and *you're* going to get it out of him!"

With an abrupt motion he shoved past Cleo, heading for the door.

"Wait a minute, Gene," Harry said. He reached out to take hold of him, but Freeman whirled without warning, swinging his left fist. He caught Harry against the temple and dropped him like an ox.

Cleo ran to the companionway. "Casey! *Casey!*"

"What's wrong? Max?"

"It's Gene! He's gone crazy! "

Casey quickly hung the wheel becket over a spoke, pulled his right arm free of the restraining sling, and made his way to the companionway. He dropped down into the galley, only to see that Freeman was waiting for him. There was a crazed glint in the man's eyes. In his hand was a half-filled whiskey bottle which he swung around in a short arc, aimed at Casey's head.

Stribling threw himself aside, partially deflecting the bottle. It glanced off his shoulder and shattered against the bulkhead, shards of glass showering over the floor and Harry's inert form.

"Gene!" Casey yelled in a futile effort to reason with Freeman. "Gene! *Wait!*"

But Freeman had taken up a long boning knife from a drawer in the galley, ready to renew his attack. Casey brought his wounded arm around in a short jab. He struck Freeman's knife arm and the knife spun up through the open companionway into the cockpit. Freeman started up after it, but a sudden heeling of the unmanned schooner sent him sprawling to the deck, sliding over the broken glass.

He screamed out in rage and pain, but immediately regained his footing and darted for the companionway steps. Casey was a yard behind him when they reached the deck. The knife lay in the cockpit well and Freeman flung himself at it. He faced around quickly, the knife held menacingly before him.

Casey stopped short at the end of the cockpit. "Gene, put it down!"

"I'm going to kill you, Stribling. I'm going to kill you right *now!*"

He came at Casey, low, slashing across with the knife, the front of his shirt torn and bloody. Casey dropped to his knees and rolled toward Freeman. He hit him at the shins, Freeman, off balance, went across the deck. He struck against the rail and, with a cry, topped over into the foaming sea.

At that same moment, Cleo pulled herself up the companionway. Casey grabbed the wheel and threw the helm hard over. The schooner turned heavily, rounding slowly, ponderously into the wind. Three-quarters of the way around, the sails began to luff, flapping noisily.

"Can you see him?" Casey called above the sound.

"I—I think so!" Cleo pointed ahead, off the port bow. "*Casey!* There's something there."

"Hold the wheel! Hold it dead ahead!"

He leaned, started the engine, then ran forward to the mast. He loosened the halyard and the mainsail came down, piling over the cabin top and into the cockpit. Cleo pushed the sail aside so that she could see where Freeman was. Casey moved on to the foremast, and the jib and foresail came down.

"What is it?" Cleo inquired when Casey returned to the cockpit. "There he is," she said, pointing to the head bobbing in the whitecaps. Just then there was a great splash near Freeman and the head disappeared abruptly.

"My God!" Casey breathed. *"Sharks!"*

"Oh, *no!"*

The head reappeared and Casey grabbed the wheel. He advanced the throttle and the heavy boat pushed ahead.

"Take a look below and see if Harry's come around!"

Cleo went to the companionway, looked down, then turned and shook her head. "Marla's down there with him. He's conscious but—"

"All right," Casey interrupted. "Come here and hold the wheel. Try to bring the boat alongside him and I'll see if I can haul him aboard."

Cleo took the wheel. Casey went to the cabin top and unlashed the long boat hook, then hurried forward on the portside.

The dorsal fin of a shark broke the surface a half dozen yards from Freeman, heading directly toward him. His hoarse scream reached the boat, and Cleo shuddered convulsively.

"Reverse, Cleo! " Casey yelled.

She pulled the lever up and pushed on the throttle. The little auxiliary roared beneath the deck, and gradually the boat lost way. Casey leaned far out with the boat hook, holding onto a stay of the foremast with his other hand.

Cleo could not see what was happening in the water. All she could see was Casey pushing out with the long-handled boat hook, and, at last, pulling back against the shroud and dropping to the deck to lean over toward the water.

"*Cleo!*" he yelled. "Need some ... help up here!"

He obviously had hold of Freeman. Cleo put the engine into neutral and the schooner fell a little off the seas and began to take on a lazy, pitching roll. Something fell below-decks with a crash.

She made her way along the deck, the salty breeze pulling at her hair. Before she got to the forward part of the deck she could hear Freeman. He was moaning and crying.

Casey called her. "Lean over beside me! Try to get hold of his arm."

She did as he directed. The upper part of Freeman's body was all that was visible beside the rolling schooner, but she could see blood about his shoulders. The sea washed it away and blood welled again from the torn flesh. A few yards out a shark broke the surface.

"Hurry!" Casey said tightly. "Come on, pull! They'll be over here after him in a second! "

Together they lifted him from the water. He seemed surprisingly light to Cleo as they dragged him over the gunwale and, as soon as they had him on deck, she saw why. His left leg was gone. His right arm had been taken off just at the elbow.

The shock hit her like a fist, and she turned away quickly with a startled cry. Her stomach knotted and she leaned over the rail, gagging.

"Cleo," Casey said gently. "I need you, Cleo."

"All right." She squeezed the stanchion tightly and turned back. She looked directly into Gene Freeman's eyes. She was amazed to see that he was still alive and conscious.

"Get Marla up here!" Casey barked. "Bring the aid kit, whatever you can find. Get sheets off the bunk—"

"No," Freeman said. "Cleo—I—"

"Get Marla. *Quick*," Casey said.

"Please..." Freeman said. "Too late. Wanta tell you—Mobley—I paid him." His face wrenched in agony, but he went on. "Told him Harry—mistreated you. Mobley do anything for—Cleo..."

"That was you last night?" Casey asked.

"Yes. Didn't want hurt—Cleo..."

"Don't talk any more, Gene," Cleo said softly.

"Not much—time. I took Max—under wharf—had to search—maybe chance to kill you, Stribling...kill you...what you did to me... *kill you*—"

Suddenly his neck arched, his head went back, and then the mangled body slackened.

Casey lowered him to the deck. He let out a slow breath and looked up at Cleo. "I guess he had it coming."

She stared blankly down at the dead man, and then she shook her head. "But not this way. Oh, God, not *this* way . .

The *Antares* lay quietly at her mooring on the quay in St. Ursula. The excitement of the schooner's arrival had passed, the bodies of the two men had been taken away, and up and down the quay business went on as usual.

Harry stood in the companionway and ran his hands tiredly through his hair. "Well, it's over. All over. And I guess Gene was right about one thing. I'll be lucky now to get away from here with my hide." He slammed a hand down on the cabin top. "To hell with it! I'm going to get drunk. I'm going to get drunker than I ever got before."

"There's a great little place for it," Marla said, pointing ashore. "Right next door to my office. I've always found it very handy."

Harry lifted himself to the deck. He took out his billfold, thumbed through the thin sheaf of currency. "The last of the Gregory fortune. Sixty-three dollars." He glanced at his wife. "Coming, Cleo? Stribling? Marla? I'll drink alone if I have to."

Cleo shook her head.

"There's work here," Casey said.

Marla came to Harry's side, smiled at him, and took his arm. "Let's go! "

"Harry!" Cleo called.

He turned. "What?"

"Harry, I—" She shook her head. "Nothing. Never mind."

She watched them walk across the quay and down the cobbled street, then she turned and went below. In the galley she put the kettle on for coffee. Should she forget what Max told her? Hadn't this thing caused enough trouble already?

Casey came down the companionway.

"Coffee?" Cleo asked him.

"Not right now. Cleo, what are you going to do?"

"About what?"

"About yourself. About you and Harry."

She drew in a breath, started to say something, then threw herself against him. "Oh, Casey, *Casey!*"

His arms went around her, pulling her to him. Suddenly, in his arms, everything seemed fine. She lifted her face, her lips seeking his, her hands moving feverishly up his back and to his shoulders. As her hand reached his shoulder she felt him wince and she pulled back quickly.

"Casey! I'm sorry! Your shoulder."

Grinning, he pulled her to him again. "To hell with the shoulder."

Her lips opened to his kiss, and the demanding urgency of her passion rose in her like a tide, all-encompassing, overwhelming. She guided his hand beneath her blouse, her breath caught as his fingers moved over her breast.

"Casey … "

"I know." His voice was husky, flat, as he picked her up and moved through the opening into the main cabin. He lowered her gently to the port bunk. "I've spent God knows how many hours lying here thinking about you, Cleo. No more thinking … "

One by one, the buttons came loose. She shrugged the blouse back over her shoulders. She pushed her hands down at the waistband of the shorts she wore, slipping them over the flare of her hips, working them down.

She lay naked, her body alive and pulsating beneath his touch. His face hovered over her, the world vanished. She arched her body to meet him, slowly, rhythmically. Eternity became compressed into an instant. Her whole being lifted in a brilliant burst, a great climactic chord. And then she drifted ... drifted ... through high clouds and snowcapped peaks, drowsily ...

"Don't go ... " she said.

"I'd like to stay here forever, but I'm afraid it can't be done."

Casey rose from the bunk. She watched him go across to the galley, his body sun-bronzed and lean. He came back and sat down beside her. He handed her a coffee mug.

She looked into his eyes, trying to read what thoughts lay there. "Casey ... " She gulped the coffee and sat up. "Hand me my clothes. I want to find Harry. There's something I've got to tell him."

"Something to tell Harry?"

She nodded quickly, her eyes sparkling. "I've been trying to decide whether to tell him or not. And now I've decided!" She picked up her scattered clothes, stood, turned her body proudly once, and began to dress.

CHAPTER THIRTEEN

H ARRY was indeed living up to his word. In less than an hour he had succeeded in bringing himself to a state wherein he found it very difficult to comprehend what was being said.

"Go away," Marla said, trying to fend Cleo off. Marla was running him a close second. "Leave him alone. You don't understand Harry."

Cleo ignored her. She sat down and looked into Harry's face. "I'm trying to tell you. It's *not* all over." She glanced around quickly, but the bar was nearly empty. Leaning closer, she went on, "Max told me how he marked the money, Harry. He *told* me!"

"Marked the money ... " he said, trailing off weakly.

But Marla seemed to understand. She got up and took Harry's arm. "Let's get him out of here."

Casey got the other arm and the four of them managed to get back to the quay and aboard the schooner. A pot of black coffee later, a bleary-eyed Harry was listening intently to Cleo.

"He said there was a cross made of stones, and the money was buried twenty paces from it, toward the beach."

Harry glanced at Casey. "How about it? Have you ever run across anything like that around the islands?"

"No. But with what we've already covered, and with all of us knowing what we're looking for, I don't see why we can't find it."

The excitement was a balm for all that had gone on before. Fresh supplies were loaded aboard the schooner after Casey had been told, and before dusk the *Antares* had cleared the harbor at St. Ursula once more and was beating her way through the islands.

Casey sailed on until dark, and hove to in the lee of an island, waiting for the moon to come up. By moonlight, they went on, making for the island where the search had ended before.

The anchorage was made about two hours before dawn, Harry and Casey sailing the boat while the women slept. Even though he'd only had a few hours sleep since leaving St. Ursula, Harry was up at daybreak, waking everyone, gathering the equipment and supplies for the day's work.

The days passed swiftly. Harry, completely consumed by the fever of the search, would allow no hour of daylight to go unused. The four of them tramped island after island in search of Max's cross. Even Casey, who was perhaps in the best physical condition of the lot, grew weary.

The bone-weariness served Cleo in one respect; it kept her thoughts off Casey as she lay in her bunk in the forepeak.

On the morning of the fifth day of the renewed search, as they sat at breakfast in the pre-dawn darkness, Marla looked around at the others.

"What do you say we take a day off?"

Harry shook his head vehemently.

"Half a day?" Marla ventured.

Harry chewed his food rapidly, hurrying to get done with it. He pointed his fork at Marla. "You stay aboard if you're tired."

"Oh, no! I've come along this far and when the treasure —if there really is one—is found, little Marla wants to be there to see it! "

"Harry," Casey said seriously, "it might do us good to take a short rest. We've been at this fourteen, fifteen hours a day now for four days."

Harry aimed the fork again, his eyebrows raised. "And look at the ground we've covered!"

"Sure. But what's the hurry?"

For Cleo there was a hurry. "I agree with Harry," she said.

Harry laughed. "Support from an unexpected quarter! I'll tell you, though, let's see what we can cover today, and if we don't turn it up, tomorrow morning we rest. Okay?"

It was agreeable to all. Breakfast finished, they rowed ashore. Cleo sat in the stern of the skiff and watched the jagged outline of the island emerge in the dawn. The pristine beauty of the islands never palled, but seemed to grow.

Through the morning they made their way along the shore, pausing only for water from the canteens, or the inevitable calls of nature.

At midmorning, Marla sat down on an outcropping of rock. "I'm bushed. Go on, I'll catch up."

Harry made no offer to hold up the search, but as they went on, Marla called, "Cleo? Got a minute?"

Cleo, puzzled, came back to where Marla was sitting. The men went on ahead, Harry covering the ground like a beagle on the scent of a rabbit.

"What is it?" Cleo said warily.

"It's about Casey—"

"Look, Marla, don't start that again!"

The older woman laughed. She took off one shoe and began to massage her foot. "I've been watching you, Cleo. You can't keep your eyes off him. And Casey's got it, too. A blind man could see the way you two look at each other. But then Harry *is* a blind man. This dough of Max's has blinded him."

"What are you getting at, Marla?"

"That's just it, doll. I'm not getting at anything. I'm throwing in the towel." Marla took off her other shoe and rubbed the foot. "I'm apologizing for what happened between us the other day. I acted like a bitch."

"Marla, I—"

"Don't misunderstand me!" She began to put the shoes on again. "I'm not being a good guy! I just know when the fight's over." She tied the shoes and stood, smiling at Cleo. "And I think I know why you're so hell-bent on finding the money, so let's get on with it!"

They caught up with the men a few minutes later. Casey looked around and for a moment his eyes met Cleo's. It was as Marla had said. Even a blind man could have seen it. It was like nothing Cleo had ever known. She longed to be with him again, to feel her body merged with his.

They went on for another hour. Cleo paused and unscrewed the cap of her canteen. She took a swallow of water and, as she lowered the canteen, saw the stones at her feet. They were overgrown with grass, but there was something symmetrical, something unnatural about their alignment.

She felt her heartbeat quicken as she knelt, brushing aside the undergrowth. "Harry! Harry!"

To her right, he stopped and looked at her. Casey and Marla paused. They all converged on Cleo.

"I'm not sure," she said. "They're partially covered. They look as though they've been here forever."

"This might be it," Harry said cautiously. He hacked away at the undergrowth with his machete. "Yes. *Look*—it's a cross. This is it! It's Max's marker!" His voice shook. "See, Stribling? This is *it!*"

Casey nodded. "I believe it is."

"*Believe* it is? Look! It's a cross—" Harry broke off quickly and looked toward the beach. "Twenty paces—that's what he said, Cleo? He said twenty paces?"

She nodded.

"Okay. Okay." Briskly Harry began to pace off the distance, counting aloud. When he reached twenty he stopped and looked around at the others. He smiled nervously and dropped his light pack to the ground. He unfastened the camping spade. "We ought to break a bottle of champagne or something!" he said.

"Come on, Harry," Cleo said. "Start digging. Let's see if it's here."

"Sure. Sure." He put the blade on the earth, pushed it in with one foot. Marla, Casey and Cleo gathered around as the hole began to deepen. He went down two feet. Three. When he was nearly waist deep he paused. Perspiration covered his face, dripping from his chin.

"I'll take it awhile," Casey said for the second time.

Harry shook his head curtly. "Cleo—" He stopped to get his breath. "Cleo, he didn't say how deep this goddamn thing was?"

"I told you everything. He barely got that much out."

Harry started to resume digging, then he pulled himself up and sat on the edge of the hole. "Maybe you had better take it, Casey."

At a depth of six feet, Casey stopped. He climbed out of the hole. "I don't see why they would have gone any deeper than that."

Harry blinked. The muscles in his jaw twitched. "It's not here. Max was a liar—"

"Take it easy, Harry!" Casey interrupted him. "We just missed the spot. You paced off twenty yards from the cross. He didn't tell Cleo whether it was from the front of it, the middle, the side—"

"That's *right!*" Harry agreed, brightening. "We'll start another hole!" He grabbed the spade from Casey, moved to the right of the hole, and began again.

There were three deep holes in the earth when they stopped for lunch. Cleo unpacked the sandwiches and they moved to the shade of a dump of palms to escape the midday sun.

"Why the hell wasn't he more exact?" Harry said angrily.

"He was dying," Cleo said. "We're lucky to be this close."

"It's just a matter of time," Marla put in.

After eating, the distance was paced off anew. Harry, stripped to the waist, began spading up the earth. Hip deep in it, he paused to take a drink of water. Cleo handed him the canteen. After he had taken a long swallow, he looked around at the three faces.

"Maybe somebody beat us to it." He wiped his mouth on the back of his hand. "The guys who put it here. Max said he hadn't been alone. He said some seamen came ashore off the U-boat with him. *They* knew where this was! One of them might have come back here after the war!"

Casey shook his head. "Max didn't even know what islands they were in until the skipper told him later. If Max was an officer and didn't know where he was, the enlisted men certainly couldn't have known."

"Harry," Cleo interrupted suddenly. She knelt quickly, looking down into the hole at Harry's feet. "Harry, isn't that something there?"

He looked down. "What—" He squatted in the hole, pawing at the earth with his hands. "Hey! It is something!" He grabbed the spade and, in a matter of seconds, lifted a dark square object up from the hole. With shaking hands, he placed it on the ground. It was surprisingly small, cube-shaped, about a foot square.

"That's it," Harry said. He jumped out of the hole, staring at the object before him. "It was here." His voice was filled with amazement, as if for the first time he really believed Max Heinrich's story.

"Is that all of it?" Cleo asked.

Harry dropped to his knees and began to tear at the heavy oilskin that was wrapped about the package. He stopped, searched his pockets futilely, then looked up quickly at Casey. "Give me your knife. *Hurry!*"

Casey handed him the knife and Harry cut away the wrapping. He tore loose the oilskin at one corner and, in the bright tropical sunlight, they all saw the tightly wrapped packet of hundred-dollar bills.

Cleo sat in the cockpit with Casey. The sails stood sheeted out, wing and wing, as the schooner ran free before the trade wind, bound for St. Ursula.

"Well, you got what you came for," Casey said quietly, glancing up intently at the sails.

Cleo nodded and turned away. Through the open companionway she could see Harry below in the main cabin, sitting at the table with Marla, happily counting the money again.

"Will you be leaving soon?"

"I—I don't know, Casey. It depends."

"I love you, Cleo,' he said huskily. "That's about all there is to it. I can't offer you the things Harry can but I'll have a pretty fair share out of this."

She felt her heartbeat quicken and she turned and looked into his eyes. He sat there at the helm, moving the wheel back and forth, expectant, like a little boy waiting for something.

"Do you—do you really love me, Casey? It wasn't just the—well, all this?" She waved her hand around at the boat and the sea and the islands.

"I can't think of anything but you, Cleo."

"It's the same with me, my darling."

"You like it here, I know. It's a great life. We could get a house up in the hills in St. Ursula."

She laughed gaily and her face grew puckish. "Is this a proposal or a proposition?"

He grinned. "Maybe I shouldn't propose to a woman who's already married, but that's what I'm doing. I want you, Cleo. All the way."

Marla came up the companionway, laughing. Harry followed her, his face flushed with excitement. He had a bottle of Max's brandy in one hand, paper cups in the other.

"It came out exactly the same! Two *million* dollars! Max knew what he was talking about! "

He sat down opposite Cleo and passed the cups around, then he poured brandy into them.

"A toast to Max Heinrich, our benefactor!" Harry raised his cup, grinning.

"To Max," Cleo said. "After all, poor Max went through—"

Harry's face darkened and he nodded. "Yeah. The poor guy." He looked across at Cleo. "Well, I guess we can pick up where we left off now. Back to the States."

"Harry..." She looked toward Casey, then drew herself up. "I'm going to do what I said, Harry. We found the money, and I'm going to leave you. I'm staying in the islands."

"You're *what?*"

"I want a divorce, Harry. It's that simple."

"You must be *kidding!* The money! I've got money again, Cleo! We can start over, live the way we used to live! "

"Maybe that's one reason I'm leaving you." She lifted her cup and drank. She could feel Casey's eyes on her.

Marla broke the silence by reaching for the bottle. "Come on, Harry, drink up! A man worth two million bucks shouldn't frown that way!"

He continued to stare at Cleo in puzzlement, then he turned to Marla, a weak smile crossing his face. "That's right—two million. What's there to frown about?" He finished his drink, poured another for Marla and for himself.

"Less five per cent," Casey reminded him gently.

Harry laughed. "Less five per cent for you." He looked at Marla and added, "And the same for Max's nurse."

Marla moved to Harry's side.

Cleo looked at them for a moment, thinking, *Maybe she'll have better luck than I did.*

The mail boat stood like a naval architect's nightmare at the quayside, the whistle blowing hoarsely, signaling imminent departure. Cleo held her hand out to Harry.

"Good-bye—and good luck."

He smiled and shook her hand. "Good-bye, Cleo. And the same to you."

"Come on, Harry!" Marla called. "We'll miss the boat!" She wore a new dress, and her hair was done up. She looked like any tourist.

They went aboard the boat. Amid a babel the gangway was pulled up and the boat eased away from the quay.

For several minutes Casey and Cleo stood quietly at the quayside, watching the boat move slowly across the harbor.

There goes the past, Cleo told herself. *There go twenty-eights years of clawing and hanging on and hoping for something good to come out of all of it.*

"Come on," Casey said, taking her arm, breaking into her thoughts.

"Where are we going?" She looked around into his swarthy, uncomplicated face.

He pointed down the quay to the schooner. "Home."

Cleo laughed, a deep sense of happiness rising up within her. She lifted his hand impulsively and kissed the tips of his fingers.

"Let's go," she said, tears suddenly blurring her sight. "Let's go home."

The End

www.ingramcontent.com/pod-product-compliance
Lightning Source LLC
Chambersburg PA
CBHW052009240626
47153CB00008B/2801